S0-ASB-404

THE FOLLOWERS

Before there was the Phantom Menace, there was . . .

JEDI APPRENTICE

STAR WARS

JEDI APPRENTICE
Special Edition

The Followers

Jude Watson

LUCAS BOOKS

SCHOLASTIC INC.

New York Toronto London Auckland Sydney
Mexico City New Delhi Hong Kong Buenos Aires

If you purchased this book without a cover, you should be aware that
this book is stolen property. It was reported as "unsold and destroyed"
to the publisher, and neither the author nor the publisher has received
any payment for this "stripped book."

No part of this publication may be reproduced in whole or in part, or
stored in a retrieval system or transmitted in any form or by any means,
electronic, mechanical, photocopying, recording, or otherwise, without
written permission of the publisher. For information regarding permission, write to Scholastic Inc., Attention: Permissions Department, 557
Broadway, New York, NY 10012.

ISBN 0-439-13939-2

Copyright © 2002 Lucasfilm Ltd. & ™. All Rights Reserved. Used Under
Authorization.

SCHOLASTIC and associated logos are trademarks and/or registered
trademarks of Scholastic Inc.

12 11 10 9 8 7 6 5 4 3   2 3 4 5 6 7/0

Printed in the U.S.A.
First Scholastic printing, April 2002

CHAPTER 1

The hologram flickered and the ghostly figures of Bant Eerin and her new Jedi Master Kit Fisto appeared in the Temple map room. Qui-Gon Jinn studied Bant's image carefully, looking directly at her silvery eyes. He was glad to see the sensitive Mon Calamarian Padawan again. Not only was she a good friend of his own eighteen-year-old apprentice, Obi-Wan Kenobi, but ever since the death of her Master Tahl years ago, Qui-Gon found himself feeling protective of her.

Bant and Qui-Gon had both suffered when Tahl died, and both still felt the loss. Qui-Gon knew Bant had continued her training despite her grief.

But she still does not seem herself, Qui-Gon thought.

Looking closer, Qui-Gon saw that there was something in Bant's eyes that was not quite right. It wasn't the profound sadness he'd grown used to seeing when Bant mourned at the Temple, when the pain was still fresh. This was something else. It took Qui-Gon a second to recognize the emotion.

It was fear. Bant was afraid. The question was, of what?

"Hello Master Qui-Gon, Obi-Wan," Kit Fisto greeted the team, bowing slightly so that some of his yellow-green head tendrils fell forward around his shoulders. "I have heard much about you from my Padawan. I am pleased to have the opportunity to speak with you, though I am afraid what we will be discussing will not be pleasant."

Qui-Gon and Obi-Wan had been summoned by the Council the day before. Nobody had told them why they were to meet Bant and Kit Fisto. Since Kit Fisto was contacting them from the largely deserted planet of Korriban, Qui-Gon had at first assumed that the task would be routine.

It only took one look at Bant's expression to know that this would not be so.

The Sith. Qui-Gon had heard stories about the Sith since he was a young boy. Every generation of initiates at the Temple knew Sith stories and legends. They thrilled in telling them to one another late at night when they should have been sleeping. Qui-Gon's generation had been no exception.

Although the stories were terrifying enough to have kept young Qui-Gon awake on more than a few nights, he had always felt that they were largely invented — myths designed to scare and not inform. Even after studying Sith history and learning that the Sith *had* existed and had been powerful, Qui-Gon remained skeptical.

But his recent conversation with Jedi Master Kit Fisto forced Qui-Gon to reexamine his beliefs about the Sith.

"Master, do you believe —" Obi-Wan hesitated.

"Do I believe in the Sith?" Qui-Gon finished his apprentice's question before answering it. Clearly Kit Fisto's report had opened up questions for Obi-Wan as well.

"Of course I do. You and I have both studied their history enough to know that the Sith threat was once very real. But we also know that they were a culture that could not survive. They killed themselves off long ago. The question remaining is whether or not they pose a current threat." Now it was Qui-Gon who hesitated.

"How can they pose a threat if they no longer exist?" Obi-Wan asked.

"The danger lies not in the Sith themselves, but in their teachings, and the ability of those teachings to inspire others to evil. As long as the Sith teachings survive, there is a potential threat."

"And if someone is spreading those teachings . . ." Obi-Wan trailed off. Qui-Gon knew he must be thinking about what Kit Fisto and Bant had found on Korriban. How could he forget the look of terror on Bant's face as she described the horrors she and her Master had seen in the valley? Or Kit Fisto's dark eyes as he told them about the dwelling they had found . . . and its chilling contents?

Inside the crude shack were tomes of Sith lore and models of ancient Sith weapons. It appeared that someone had been compiling every scrap of information to be found about the Sith, both truth and myth. And scrawled on one wall was a crude drawing of a Sith Holocron beside a message written in Sith code. *Location known. Follow the leader.*

A simple Holocron was not necessarily dangerous. The crystal information-storage devices were even used by the Jedi. Palm-sized and easy to transport, Holocrons were an excellent way to store vast amounts of knowledge.

But the Jedi Holocrons that Qui-Gon had seen were square. The Holocron drawing on Korriban was pyramid-shaped, a formation unique to the Sith. And the knowledge contained in a Sith Holocron was infinitely more dangerous. It focused on dark power and how to gain, use, and manipulate it.

If one existed, and if it fell into the wrong hands, a Sith Holocron could be more than deadly.

"We have knowledge of several Sith Sects operating in the galaxy," Jedi Archivist Jocasta Nu reported. "We monitor them, but until now they have never given us much cause for alarm. They've never gained large followings, and their activities are not unlike those of other small criminal groups. They have always been more of a nuisance than a threat."

Though it had taken him a little while to get used to working with her, Jocasta Nu was beginning to grow on Qui-Gon. He generally did not like to use the usual channels for obtaining information. But he'd come to appreciate Jocasta's straightforward manner. She never failed to provide Qui-Gon with the information he needed.

"Lately there has been increased activity at one of the higher learning institutions right here on Coruscant," Jocasta said. "According to our sources, this is due to a professor named Murk Lundi." She flashed an image of the Quermian professor onto a screen.

It was not the first time Qui-Gon had heard of Professor Lundi. An infamous galaxy historian, Lundi was popular with students and admired by his colleagues. Qui-Gon had even heard him called one of the finest historians of the era. But he did not understand what Lundi had to do with the dwelling found on Korriban.

"For the past several years Lundi has been narrowing his focus," Jocasta explained. "Now all of his research and lectures revolve around the dark side of the Force. As his focus has narrowed, his student following has grown."

Jocasta pushed several student texts toward Qui-Gon and Obi-Wan. There were posters for Sith rallies and hand-drawn story strips showing Sith battles. "His classes are among the most popular on campus. His texts are so sought after they are difficult for students to obtain." She paused for a moment. "But there were several of them among the items found on Korriban."

So that's it, Qui-Gon thought. *The Council believes one of Dr. Lundi's followers gathered the information that was found on Korriban.*

Qui-Gon looked up to find Obi-Wan already gazing at him knowingly. Neither of the Jedi needed to say a word — their next move was clear.

It was time for a crash-course on the Sith.

CHAPTER 2

Obi-Wan pushed his way through the crowd of students and toward the back of the room without worrying about being spotted. It was not hard to lose himself in the throng.

The students on Coruscant were so varied that you would have had to be on fire to get even a second glance. Besides, Obi-Wan and his Master were the only ones not desperately pushing forward, trying to get a word with Professor Lundi before class started.

From his spot against the wall, Obi-Wan could just make out the Quermian teacher's head swaying slightly on its long neck in the middle of the crowd. Apart from his advanced years and the small black apparatus covering one of his eyes, Murk Lundi looked a lot like the Jedi Master Yarael Poof. He was the same species, and had the same commanding presence. But there was something very different about Dr. Lundi, something chilling that Obi-Wan couldn't put his finger on.

Across the room, Qui-Gon was also watching the professor, his eyes narrowed in steady focus. Had he noticed something else? In the din Obi-Wan considered contacting Qui-Gon on his comlink to hear his thoughts. But at that moment Dr. Lundi raised several of his arms, signaling that class was about to start.

More quickly than Obi-Wan could have imagined, the hoard of students found seats and the room fell silent. The course hall was enormous, yet every chair was taken. Every spot to stand or lean or sit was filled by a student, and at least a dozen hovercams recorded the professor's every word for the students who could not fit inside the room.

Obi-Wan surveyed the crowd. Not only was the turnout impressive, but each student sat with rapt attention. After half an hour they remained riveted — there was no sign of drifting or feeling drowsy. Obi-Wan had hoped to spot a few students who seemed unusually drawn in or somehow conspicuous. As it turned out, *he* was the conspicuous one for looking around while the professor was speaking.

At the front of the room, Dr. Lundi paced in the narrow space not taken up by students. Taking small steps on his long legs, his body seemed to float as he spoke. Every now and then he paused, clearly enjoying his position and his ability to make the crowd hold its breath in anticipation of his every thought.

Murk Lundi was not at all like the teachers Obi-Wan had at the Temple. In the Temple, Obi-Wan's instructors were like partners in learning, guides who wanted to help him discover things for himself and not just force their own opinions.

Obi-Wan did not appreciate the learning style he was seeing today. Yet the more he listened to Dr. Lundi, the more he wanted to hear. Soon he, too, was waiting for the professor's next word.

"No being besides the Sith themselves has ever seen a Sith Holocron. There are rumors. Yes. There are also drawings and legends and myths. However, most historians believe that the Sith were so protective of their knowledge that they destroyed it themselves before letting it fall to the unworthy. After all, we are talking about beings who killed their Masters when they had learned all they could from them." Lundi paused and looked at his students with a sly smile. "Should I be nervous about graduation day?" Then he went on.

"Some scholars contend that the Sith did not

use Holocrons at all, that they would not have been so foolish as to store so much power in a crystal that I could hold in my hand." The professor paused, gazing at one of his outstretched palms. "More power than this galaxy has known in a long, long time.

"However, if there is one thing I have learned from my lifelong study of history, it is this: Every myth is based on a small seed of truth. One has to delve deeply to find it. But it is there, below the surface, waiting to be discovered."

Obi-Wan was not sure how much time had passed before he forced himself to close his eyes and bring his mind back to the task at hand. Murk Lundi made the Sith more real than any late-night ghost story, but that was not why Obi-Wan was here. He had to stay focused.

But by succumbing, even for a short time, Obi-Wan understood Murk Lundi's hold over his students. Dr. Lundi's fascinating subject was made even more so by his own intelligence and charisma. Lundi's power over the students was impressive. And more than that, it was dangerous. Lundi's students seemed likely to believe anything their teacher said without question, and the way he spoke about the dark side made it sound enticing. Could they be inspired to delve too deeply?

Obi-Wan focused once more on the students. It had to be one of them, or someone like them, who had assembled the Sith lore on Korriban.

A small group in the first row captured Obi-Wan's attention. The four students sat front and center, leaning forward whenever the professor spoke.

The first, a dark-haired humanoid, nodded at the end of each of Lundi's statements. Next to him, a redheaded boy was so riveted that he held his hands just above his desk as if he had been about to fold them in his lap but froze when the professor began to speak. The third boy was transcribing every word on a datapad, in spite of the fact that he had his own small hovercam recording the entire lecture. Last was a girl who clung protectively to a coat and document case that Obi-Wan guessed belonged to Dr. Lundi.

Suddenly a yellow light went on over the desk of the dark-haired boy in the front row. Obi-Wan quickly realized that the light alerted the professor that a student wished to ask a question.

Dr. Lundi stopped in mid-sentence. His head swiveled on its long neck, and Obi-Wan caught an angry gleam in the Quermian's uncovered eye. But the anger disappeared when the professor saw who had dared to interrupt him. The humanoid boy was obviously a favorite. Dr. Lundi even called him by name.

"Yes, Norval?" he asked.

Norval stood. "Please forgive the interruption, professor. I only want to know if it is true that the Sith were more powerful than the Jedi."

Dr. Lundi laughed lightly, as if Norval's question was childish. "Of course," he said. "Power and vengeance are much stronger motives than peace could ever be. The Sith could have easily controlled the entire galaxy had they not made their one mistake —"

Dr. Lundi was interrupted by a tone signaling the end of class.

Students sat silently in their seats, hoping the professor would finish his thought. But Dr. Lundi was already collecting his coat and case from the girl in the front row.

"There will be no class next week," the professor announced. The class groaned. Lundi smiled at their disappointment. "I am taking a small sabbatical."

Yellow lights went on over desks throughout the room.

"When I return I may have exciting information to share with you." Dr. Lundi smirked mysteriously. "Until then, my assistant Dedra will answer any after-class questions."

The girl who had been holding the professor's things stood at the front of the room. Obi-Wan thought she looked overwhelmed as Dr. Lundi moved smoothly out of the course hall followed by Norval and the redheaded boy, who Norval called Omal. Obi-Wan noticed that the redheaded boy had bright, sharp-looking eyes. He was clearly excited, and talked animatedly with Norval about the lecture.

Obi-Wan and Qui-Gon exchanged a glance before they, too, made their way toward the door and slipped out of the hall. It looked as though they would be taking a little sabbatical of their own.

CHAPTER 3

Qui-Gon would have liked to stay and talk to the students in Dr. Lundi's class, but the professor's surprise announcement changed everything. Dr. Lundi was up to something, and the most important thing was to find out what it was and where he was going.

The Quermian moved surprisingly quickly for someone his age, but the Jedi kept up easily. Qui-Gon followed Lundi into a terminal and watched him board a midsize craft. Not knowing where the transport was going, the Jedi had no choice but to follow him aboard.

Once inside the transport it became clear that the vessel was a private, no-frills charter. The main hold had been outfitted with close rows of seats filled almost to capacity. Both the seats and the passengers looked like they had seen better days.

"Are you going to Lisal?" a voice growled from a dim corner near the entrance.

"Yes," Qui-Gon answered quickly. The ship's destination sounded familiar.

"Tickets?" the voice demanded.

"Two please," Qui-Gon answered.

"It's too late to buy them now." The surly captain stepped out of the shadows to reveal his bad breath and broken teeth to the Jedi. "If you don't have any you'll have to pay double."

"We'll be happy to pay the regular fee," Qui-Gon replied, calmly looking into the pilot's beady eyes.

"Two at the regular price, then," the captain said. He reached into his vest pocket and pulled out two grimy stubs. "You'll have to sit in the back."

Obi-Wan handed the captain a few credits while Qui-Gon scanned the crowd for Murk Lundi. He was not sitting with the rest of the passengers. But with so many eyes on them the Jedi did not dare search the rest of the ship for him. At least not yet.

Obi-Wan and Qui-Gon squeezed into the back row and sat down. As he settled into his seat, Qui-Gon's knees pressed comically against the row ahead of him. There was not nearly enough room to accommodate the Jedi's large frame.

Several of the motley passengers ahead had turned to glare at them.

This is not a typical tour group, Qui-Gon noted. The passengers on the charter seemed surlier than the average pleasure travelers to Coruscant. Jocasta Nu had warned them that members of the Sith Sects might be anyone and that they would be difficult to pick out of a crowd. Suddenly Qui-Gon wondered if they had stumbled into the middle of a sect. Why had Lisal sounded so familiar?

The captain struggled to close the ship's doors. After pushing and then pounding several buttons he ripped the control panel off and began to tug on the sparking wires inside.

"I hope the engine is in better condition," Obi-Wan observed, gaining the Jedi a few more hard stares.

Qui-Gon wished he had had a little more time to reflect on how this mission was shaping up and what exactly he and his apprentice were getting into. It was all happening too quickly. This morning they had been asked to keep an eye on an influential professor, and now they were suddenly headed off-planet.

In the back of his mind Qui-Gon had a strange feeling that this trip wasn't what it appeared to be. He was suddenly filled with a feeling of foreboding. This could easily be a trap.

Qui-Gon stood. Perhaps there was still time to get off the vessel. But before he could decide what to do, the captain's swearing turned to angry shouts. Someone was screaming Dr. Lundi's name and struggling to get through the partially closed door.

It only took Qui-Gon a moment to recognize the young man trying to board. It was Norval, the dark-haired student from the front row.

The captain did his best to push the intruder back out the half-open door. Several passengers crowded around. It was not clear whether they were trying to help Norval in or help the captain force him out. Then, in a shower of sparks from the control panel, the doors suddenly opened. Norval and several passengers fell into a heap on the floor.

"You'll pay triple!" the captain bellowed, pointing at Norval and splattering him and several other passengers with spittle.

"He won't be staying," said a soft, familiar voice behind the captain. It was the professor. In the chaos Qui-Gon had not seen him appear.

"Please take me with you," Norval begged. He grabbed the edge of Dr. Lundi's robes. "You need me," he whimpered. "Nobody knows your texts as well as I do. I've studied every word. You must show me how to use the —"

"Guards," Lundi snapped. "Guards, remove this boy immediately."

Two enormous hangar guards appeared on the gangplank and pulled Norval to his feet.

"You are too old to use it on your own!" Norval continued to shriek as they pulled him out of the ship and down the ramp. "You need me!"

Murk Lundi did not move. Even after Norval's pleas had faded and the captain had succeeded in sealing the door, he still stood staring at the durasteel hatch.

Qui-Gon seized the opportunity to leave his seat. He squeezed past the distracted passengers, pulling Obi-Wan along with him. They would not be leaving the ship. The mission was more important than he'd originally thought.

It looked as though there was a Sith Holocron and Murk Lundi was going after it.

CHAPTER 4

Obi-Wan tried the door even though he did not expect it to open — none of the other doors in the corridor had. So he was surprised when this one slid easily into the wall. The stale odor that billowed from the room confirmed that although the door was unlocked, it hadn't been opened in some time. The musty room would be perfect.

After motioning to his Master, Obi-Wan stepped inside to look around. It appeared he had found an abandoned laundry room. Piles of uniforms littered the floor and stagnant water filled two large basins.

Qui-Gon wrinkled his nose when he walked in. "Good work, Obi-Wan," he said quietly as he closed the door. "No one will look for us here." Pulling his comlink from his belt, the Jedi Master contacted the Temple.

"Right to follow him, you are," Yoda said after hearing Qui-Gon's report. "Find the Holocron first, we must."

And Lundi is our only clue to finding it, Obi-Wan thought.

Bant and Kit Fisto hadn't been able to give them any ideas about where the Holocron might be located. Their best option was to follow Lundi — so they could take the Holocron from him if he found it.

Qui-Gon ended his transmission. Obi-Wan could tell that he felt the same way. Unless they knew where they were going, it would be nearly impossible to get to the Holocron first.

"We need more information," Qui-Gon muttered, reactivating his comlink. A moment later Jocasta Nu's voice echoed in the small room.

"There have been rumors of Sith Holocrons in existence in several places across the galaxy. Lisal, Korriban, Kodai, Doli. Most of the claims have been investigated by Jedi teams, but nothing has ever been found."

"Thank you, Jocasta," Qui-Gon said. "As usual you have been helpful."

"I'm always here to assist with information. Feel free to contact me should you need anything else," Jocasta replied.

"Of course." Qui-Gon signed off and turned to his Padawan. "Lundi must be looking for the Lisal Holocron," he said.

That's too easy, Obi-Wan thought. "We need to know more. I'm going to find Lundi," the Padawan said. He stripped off the tunic he'd worn to blend in with the students.

"Patience, Obi-Wan," Qui-Gon reprimanded quietly. "It will take time for things to unfold."

Obi-Wan knew his Master was right. But frustration was welling up inside of him. He kicked at the pile of uniforms at his feet until he saw one that looked about his size. After holding it against his shoulders, he pulled it on. It fit well enough.

"We will not discover anything tonight," Qui-Gon said. "We must give Lundi time to relax, to let down his guard. Lisal is a two-day journey. We have time." Qui-Gon arranged himself on one of the cleaner laundry piles and prepared to sleep.

Obi-Wan sighed and did the same. Qui-Gon was right, he supposed. But for him, waiting was often the hardest part of a mission. It made him anxious. And when he was anxious he could not easily sleep.

Obi-Wan awoke suddenly. Something was not right. Sitting up quickly, he reached out to the Force to try and find the source of the danger he felt. When he was sure that there was no one in the laundry facility besides himself and his Master, he removed his hand from his saber hilt.

Beside him, Qui-Gon breathed steadily, either asleep or deep in meditation. Whatever had disturbed Obi-Wan did not seem to be upsetting his Master.

Obi-Wan lay back and closed his eyes to try and recapture an image of what had frightened him. Had it been a dream? A presence? Just a feeling?

Pyramid-shaped Holocrons floated in his mind. Certainly it was disturbing to think that such potent capsules were at large in the galaxy. But he did not think that was what had awakened him.

The Holocrons faded and another image grew. A figure. Obi-Wan allowed his fear to grow with the image. Then he relaxed and let the fear go, focusing on the figure. But no matter how he tried, he could not see a face. The visage remained in shadow and a feeling became clear — the feeling that someone had discovered them.

When Obi-Wan surfaced from his meditation, he saw that Qui-Gon was awake and had been aware of his agitation. "It is a warning," Qui-Gon said after Obi-Wan told him about it. "We must proceed with extra caution and find out where we are headed. Quickly."

Obi-Wan laughed when Qui-Gon emerged in the corridor wearing a mechanic's uniform. The pants stopped close to the top of his boots, and the sleeves were rolled up in an effort to disguise the fact that they were at least ten centimeters too short. But Obi-Wan had to admit that nobody would recognize Qui-Gon as a Jedi Master.

"You don't look any better," Qui-Gon chided his apprentice.

Obi-Wan knew it was true. Wearing the soiled uniform he had pulled from the pile the night before, he even *smelled* like a grubby mechanic.

"I think Lundi must have arranged for a private room. Let's separate and search the ship. We need to find him or his quarters," Qui-Gon said, getting down to business. "Do not let the captain see you."

Obi-Wan nodded and moved quietly down the corridor, away from Qui-Gon. He tried doors and reached out with his senses. Lundi had such a strong presence that Obi-Wan did not think he would be hard to find.

After a few minutes Obi-Wan saw the open doors to the ship's bridge. Pressing himself against the corridor wall, he paused and listened. The captain was at the helm, of course. But someone else was there as well.

It only took Obi-Wan a moment to realize it was Lundi. But what was he doing at the ship's controls?

Looking around, Obi-Wan quickly spotted a maintenance ladder. It led to a catwalk that trailed over the bridge and toward several hyperdrive access panels. If he pulled himself along on his stomach, and the captain and Lundi did not look up, he could get close enough to hear what they were saying. Obi-Wan climbed up.

"You don't seem to be understanding me, captain," Lundi said in a low, menacing voice. "I am not asking you to stop on Nolar. I am telling you."

"And you don't seem to understand that this ship is not going to Nolar. It's going to Lisal!" the captain bellowed. He slammed a meaty fist down on the controls, sending a small piece flying.

"But I don't need to go to Lisal," Lundi said, holding his ground.

Obi-Wan inched farther out on the catwalk until he was almost directly over Lundi and the captain.

Lundi's head moved slowly back and forth as he fiddled with something under his robe. The captain followed the Quermian's small head with his eyes.

"I will only say this once more," Lundi said, his head still swaying. "The equipment I need is on Nolar. You will stop on Nolar. I will make it *very* worth your trip."

With a great effort the captain looked away from the Quermian's face and down at the folds of the professor's robe.

Obi-Wan could barely see something sparkle in Lundi's hands — he could have had something very valuable. Whatever it was, it seemed to change the captain's mind.

"I'll stop, but I'm not waiting," the captain finally spat.

"You will not regret it," Lundi growled back.

CHAPTER 5

The ship landed on Nolar within an hour. Obi-Wan barely had time to find his Master and brief him on what he'd heard on the bridge.

After Lundi quickly disembarked on Nolar, Obi-Wan and Qui-Gon pushed their way past the puzzled captain. The Jedi followed as the professor made his way into a tiny, adjoining hangar. There was one small ship inside, and Lundi spoke briefly with its pilot before leaving the hangar.

"It looks like he just booked continuing passage," Obi-Wan said thoughtfully as the Jedi followed Lundi into the city. "But I was under the impression that Nolar was his final destination. Where do you think he's going?"

Qui-Gon let out a slow breath. "We shall soon see."

The capital city of Nolari was bustling. There was a great deal of both air and foot traffic. The city was populated by beings from many parts of the galaxy.

Obi-Wan tried to stay close to his Master, who strode purposefully ahead.

It wasn't difficult to keep track of Murk Lundi. His long neck, multiple arms, and tiny head made him an easy visual target, even in a densely populated metropolis like Nolari. But it was not long before an uneasy feeling came over Obi-Wan. He sensed that someone or something was following *them.* But what, or who?

Without slowing down, Qui-Gon turned back to his apprentice. "Stay close to me," he said quietly. "I think we are being followed."

"I feel a presence too, Master," Obi-Wan replied. "But I am not getting any sense of who it might be."

Qui-Gon began to move more quickly through the crowds. Obi-Wan was accustomed to his Master's long, powerful strides, but he found it difficult to move inconspicuously. In spite of the varied populace, their smelly mechanics' uniforms seemed to stick out.

Looking fleetingly over his shoulder, Obi-Wan suddenly spotted their pursuer — a humanoid figure wearing a long cape and a helmet.

"I see him, Master," Obi-Wan spoke quietly. "About forty paces behind us, to the right."

Qui-Gon nodded curtly. "We're going to have to split up," he said. "I will follow Murk. You should lead our new friend away from me, and then double back to see who he or she is."

Obi-Wan nodded. He looked over his shoulder a second time. By the time he cast his eyes forward again, Qui-Gon had disappeared into the throng.

Obi-Wan made a sharp left turn. Using his peripheral vision he saw his pursuer stop for an instant, as if unsure of which way to go. A moment later, he continued to follow Obi-Wan.

Relieved, Obi-Wan moved ahead. He zigzagged through a crowded marketplace, barely pausing to look at the delectable fruits and vegetables sold at various stands. Several vendors called out to him, aggressively trying to sell their foods. Obi-Wan's stomach growled. Unfortunately there was no time for a snack.

On the far side of the open market, Obi-Wan ducked behind a stack of crates. His tracker passed by quickly, but by the time Obi-Wan emerged from his hiding place he had disappeared again. Quickly scanning the crowd, Obi-Wan pressed on. But he was not able to find a lone figure in a helmet wandering the streets.

Obi-Wan was beginning to worry that he had failed his assignment when he suddenly spotted a flutter of gray fabric ahead. Hurrying forward, he saw the figure vanish around a corner.

He definitely looks humanoid, Obi-Wan thought. *But male or female?*

Obi-Wan rounded the corner quickly and nearly collided with a group of seedy-looking characters. Annoyed by the intrusion, two of the group glared openly at the Jedi. A third pulled out a blaster and leveled it at Obi-Wan's chest.

"Wrong turn," he growled. His arm was heavily bandaged above the wrist, but the heavy blaster did not waver in his hand.

Obi-Wan kept his eyes on the man's face as he pulled his lightsaber from his belt. Had he been at Dr. Lundi's lecture on Coruscant? Or on the ship? The young Jedi had been fairly sure that he and Qui-Gon were the only passengers to disembark besides the professor.

"I'm afraid this is your unlucky day," another thug spat.

Obi-Wan stepped forward slightly and ignited his lightsaber. That action alone was usually enough to intimidate an adversary. But the thugs didn't back down. In fact, now there were two blasters aimed at him.

"Ah, a lightsaber," one of the armed lowlifes mocked. "But does he use it wisely for power and vengeance, or foolishly for peace?"

The rest of the thugs smirked, and Obi-Wan's mind jolted. He'd heard those words before, and recently — at Dr. Lundi's lecture. These lowlifes were obviously familiar with Lundi and his work. Was this an ambush? Obi-Wan wanted to ask, but one of the hoodlums fired before he could get a word out.

Obi-Wan swung. Too late. The bolt grazed his shoulder, and he felt a hot pain tear through his flesh. He ignored the fierce throbbing as he leaped forward and swung again. This time he hit his target and severed a thug's finger from its hand.

The lowlife howled in pain. "You can't win, Jedi," he growled. Clutching his wounded hand, he fled deeper into the alley. His wide-eyed companions were quick to follow.

After clipping his lightsaber to his belt, Obi-Wan checked his shoulder. The throbbing had subsided. The wound was minor and would heal quickly.

By the time Obi-Wan stepped into the open street, he had lost track of his pursuer. He stood completely still for a few moments, refocusing his energy to determine which way he should go. The answer was not entirely clear.

Obi-Wan started off in a new direction, heading away from the crowded marketplace. The city center soon gave way to large, storehouse-type buildings. Obi-Wan was satisfied that his pursuer was long gone when he sensed Qui-Gon's presence. Obi-Wan stopped before one of the storehouses. Then, doubling back to the door, he ducked inside.

Obi-Wan knew immediately that his Master was not alone in the storehouse. Murk Lundi was here as well. Moving carefully behind large crates and machinery, Obi-Wan made his way toward the center of the large room. Soon he could hear two men carrying on a conversation.

"I need a Nolarian 6000 drill immediately," one of the voices said. Obi-Wan recognized it as Dr. Lundi's.

Peering out from behind a vehicle, Obi-Wan saw that Lundi was talking to a machinery dealer. The dealer was holding a large wrench and his forearms were covered in grease.

"Don't have one," the dealer said flatly. "There's a shortage. And the way the mining safety committee has been watching us, there will be for a good while."

"I need a 6000. *Today*," Lundi repeated.

The dealer sighed, as if he got requests for enormous subaquatic drill rigs all the time. "Are you listening?" he asked, annoyed. "I said I don't have one. And I don't know when I will."

Lundi stared at the man, clenching and un-clenching his many hands into fists. His face contorted into a twisted scowl.

Behind the machinery, Obi-Wan suddenly felt a little hazy. His vision blurred and the voices around him echoed in his ears. From some-where in his daze he realized that Dr. Lundi's anger was affecting him. Yoda had told Obi-Wan that anger and hatred clouded one's mind but he'd never felt this muddled by someone else's anger before. Jedi Master Yarael Poof had amazing powers of Force suggestion. Perhaps all Quermians were telepathic.

By concentrating hard, Obi-Wan was able to clear his vision and his head. He focused on what was transpiring in front of him. Lundi was now shouting at the machinery dealer.

"Pathetic weakling," he raged. "Only a fool would let such technicalities interrupt his busi-ness."

The dealer stood staring at Lundi, frozen.

Lundi turned and stormed toward the store-house door. "I have the power to find it without your stupid machinery," he told himself. His several arms waved forcefully through the air. "It is simply a matter of timing. Yes. I just have to time it right."

What does that mean? Obi-Wan wondered as

he followed Lundi out of the storehouse. His Master was not far behind, and the two Jedi stepped out into the street as if they had been together the whole time.

Lundi, however, had vanished.

CHAPTER 6

Qui-Gon noted Obi-Wan's injury as well as the scowl on his face as the young Jedi peered down the street. There was no sign of anyone. Like Obi-Wan, he was wondering where Lundi could have gone so quickly. But he had witnessed stranger disappearing acts.

Obi-Wan turned back toward his Master. His mouth was slightly open, as if he were about to say something. But at that moment a third figure fled in the opposite direction. Without so much as a nod to each other, the Jedi gave chase.

The figure retreated down an alley and disappeared into a narrow walkway between two buildings. The Jedi followed close behind, nearly colliding into a duracrete wall. A dead end.

Qui-Gon ran his fingers along the wall's surface to see if it was some kind of temporary barrier. The wall seemed permanent and solid, but the elusive figure was nowhere to be found.

"This mission is making me crazy!" Obi-Wan said, exasperated. "We're not getting anywhere!"

Qui-Gon gazed steadily at his Padawan. Then he bent to take a closer look at the boy's wounded shoulder.

"I was surrounded by a street gang," Obi-Wan said more quietly, but he couldn't keep his frustration in check. "They were looking for trouble and when they found I was a Jedi they wanted to stop me even more." Obi-Wan's voice grew louder and he pulled away from his Master. "I don't understand how there can be so many people after us when we hardly know what we are after ourselves!"

The young Jedi's response was not appropriate, of course. A Jedi Knight did not throw temper tantrums. But this mission *was* frustrating. In addition to the humiliation of being injured by a band of ruffians, Obi-Wan, he realized suddenly, was feeling anger fed by close contact with the dark side. It was essential that he be patient and guide him in the right direction. If he didn't, the boy could take a fateful turn and be lost to him forever.

"You must not let the nature of this mission disturb you so, Padawan," Qui-Gon said calmly.

"I know it is difficult. We are dealing with a powerful evil. But becoming angry only takes you a treacherous step closer to the dark side."

Obi-Wan looked down at his feet, as if ashamed of his anger.

"Anger and fear of the dark side are easy paths," Qui-Gon went on, as if Obi-Wan had spoken of his shame. "It is not difficult to let negative emotions overtake you. It *is* difficult to let them move through you and leave without reacting to them. Yet that is exactly what you must do."

Obi-Wan nodded, and Qui-Gon sensed that the boy understood in his head what he was telling him. But he also knew that it was much harder to feel it in one's heart.

Without speaking, Qui-Gon turned and left the dead-end alleyway, heading back toward the street. "Let us review what we do know," he said as he strode forward. In truth he did not feel as confident about how to proceed as he appeared. But he wanted to give his Padawan a sense of positive direction.

"We know that Dr. Lundi has a large and zealous following of students — and many others as well. There are Sith Sects throughout the galaxy and they are very likely in touch with one another. That could explain why so many people are anxious to stop us. We know Lundi is after a Sith Holocron, and that he needs difficult-to-obtain mining equipment to get it. Or at least he would have liked to have had the equipment to go after it. We also know that there is some question of timing, and whether Lundi can manage the powerful Holocron on his own."

"Those are just the rantings of a delusional student," Obi-Wan pointed out. "One who was desperate to be included on the trip."

Qui-Gon paused in his step, but only slightly. "True," he agreed. "But we have received accurate information from far stranger sources."

Obi-Wan did not respond, and Qui-Gon did not pressure him any further. The boy needed time to process his emotions.

The Jedi decided to head back to the hangar. If they moved quickly they might be able to steal aboard Dr. Lundi's newly hired ship before it departed.

Making their way back toward the market-place, Qui-Gon pulled his comlink from his utility belt. It was time to contact the Jedi Council. This mission was anything but ordinary, and he wanted to keep Yoda informed about how it was developing.

He was surprised by the information that Yoda had for *him*.

"Information about another, larger collection

of Sith items we have," Yoda said gravely. His voice was steady, but Qui-Gon sensed that the wise Jedi Master was alarmed nonetheless. "An anonymous informant it was."

Qui-Gon listened intently to everything Yoda said, pausing in the street several times. Obi-Wan slowed alongside him, his eyes registering curiosity and concern. When the transmission was finished, Qui-Gon sighed heavily. He was beginning to get a bad feeling about all of this.

"They've discovered other Sith artifacts," Qui-Gon began.

"I thought it was something like that," Obi-Wan said with a serious nod. "What did they find?"

"A whole storehouse full of partially constructed weapons and devices, and copies of Dr. Lundi's texts and teachings," Qui-Gon replied. "The trademark drawing of a Sith Holocron was on the wall."

Obi-Wan was quiet for a moment as they continued to head back to the hangar. "Where was the storehouse?" he finally asked.

"Umgul, in the Mid Rim," Qui-Gon replied. He quickened his stride slightly. The sooner they got back to the hangar, the better.

Obi-Wan kept up with his Master. "Nowhere near the first stash," he said thoughtfully.

"Exactly," Qui-Gon agreed with a nod. Though

he and his apprentice had only recently become aware of them, Sith Sect followers were becoming a hard, cold fact of life.

Qui-Gon moved past an alien selling electronic gadgets and a humanoid female pushing a loaded fruit cart.

Do they study the Sith? he wondered.

A small crowd of people suddenly appeared in front of Qui-Gon, and he momentarily lost track of his apprentice. Normally this would not have bothered him. It was impossible to keep his eyes on his Padawan at all times. But for some reason this time it was disturbing.

Before he could weave through the cluster, blaster fire rang out.

CHAPTER 7

Obi-Wan had his lightsaber activated in less than a second. But with the screaming hoards of people on all sides of him, it was difficult to tell where the bolts were coming from. Focusing his energy, he stood completely still for a nanosecond, then slashed out, ignoring the pain in his shoulder. He successfully deflected three bolts before the firing stopped.

Screams of panic echoed around him long after the firing was over. In the aftermath it was nearly impossible to be certain of the origin of the shots. Obi-Wan deactivated his lightsaber amid more screams and stares. Luckily, nobody appeared to be hurt.

Suddenly Qui-Gon was by his side again. His Master did not need to speak for Obi-Wan to know that there was no use trying to pursue their assailant. The issue at hand was finding the most direct escape route.

Qui-Gon led the way through the crowd to a secluded area outside the market. They were just getting their bearings when more blaster fire rang out — and whizzed past Obi-Wan's head, nearly grazing an ear. Obi-Wan dropped, then quickly got back on his feet. It was definitely time to return to the hangar.

As they raced through the streets, Obi-Wan wondered if life on Nolar was always this hazardous or if the Jedi had been targeted specifically. If so, by whom? The thugs in the alley? How large a network of Sith Sects could there be? And who was informing them?

Another blaster bolt whizzed past them, but it missed the Jedi by nearly a meter. They were getting away.

Obi-Wan ran after his Master. He appeared to be taking a roundabout path, probably in an attempt to lose their pursuer altogether. As they turned corners and wove through the streets, they gradually left their assailant behind.

Finally the Jedi arrived back at the hangar. Obi-Wan rushed inside and skidded to a stop, but the ship Lundi had hired was gone. Its pilot was lying in a heap on the floor.

The Jedi rushed to the pilot. His large rust-colored head lay on the ground at an odd angle. There was an ugly lump at the base of his neck, and one of his long arms was draped over his closed eyes.

Squatting down beside him, Qui-Gon took his pulse. "It's weak and slow, but it's there," he reported, sitting back on his heels.

"Do you think he's been drugged?" Obi-Wan asked, looking over the body. The pilot's two-toed feet were pointing at awkward angles.

"It looks that way," Qui-Gon replied. "As well as being struck on the head." He stood up with a sigh. "It may be several hours before we are even able to talk to him."

Obi-Wan held back his exasperation. Another roadblock. They were on an important mission, yet had no idea where they were going or what they were supposed to do. And to top it off, they were stranded on a planet with someone who wanted to stop them, possibly for good.

Trying not to let frustration overtake him completely, Obi-Wan turned his back on the pilot and sat down to wait.

Two hours later, the pilot groaned and sat up groggily. Looking around, he appeared to take in the two Jedi and the empty space where his ship had been a few hours ago. There was a moment of heavy silence before he began to shout in anger. He tried to leap to his feet, but quickly sat back down. Gingerly feeling the back of his neck, he found the lump and shouted some more.

"Try to remain calm," Qui-Gon said in a soothing tone. The pilot cursed but didn't attempt to stand up again.

"Your ship was stolen, then?" Qui-Gon asked. He got up and crossed the hangar in a few quick strides.

"Well, I don't think I *misplaced it,*" the pilot replied hotly. The sound of his voice was strange, since it came out of his two mouths at once. He eyed Qui-Gon with distrust. "Who are you?"

"I am Qui-Gon Jinn and this is my apprentice, Obi-Wan Kenobi," he replied. "We believe the being we are following may have stolen your ship. Can you tell us what happened?"

The captain gently rubbed the lump on the back of his neck. "I was working on my ship — making minor adjustments to the hyperdrive. Someone came up behind me and whacked me on the back of my neck." The pilot winced as he continued rubbing his wound.

"Did you see your attacker?" Obi-Wan asked.

The pilot shook his head. "I didn't see anyone. Or hear anything, actually. It could have been any thief or scoundrel. There are plenty around here."

"Do you think it was the being who hired passage on your ship a few hours ago? The Quermian?"

"How do you know about the Quermian?" the captain asked. But before the Jedi could reply he waved his hand through the air dismissively. "It doesn't matter. But I don't know why he'd attack the pilot who was about to take him to a place he asked to go."

"Perhaps he was interested in piloting the ship himself," Qui-Gon mused.

"Or saving the fare," Obi-Wan added.

The pilot sighed. "There are many thieves on Nolar. This kind of thing happens all the time." He looked around the empty hangar and a spark of fury came into his eyes. "Just not to me."

Obi-Wan knew how the pilot felt. He'd been frustrated with this mission pretty much since it started.

But at the moment he and Qui-Gon needed information more than anything else. He had to stay calm and focused.

"Can you tell us where you were going to take the Quermian?" he asked.

"Of course," the pilot said. Obi-Wan noticed that he seemed more willing to help the Jedi. Perhaps he thought it might get his ship back. "I had just finished keying the information into my navcomputer. I remember because it's not a planet I'm asked to fly to very often. In fact, I can't say I've ever been there."

"And the name of the planet?" Qui-Gon asked.

"Kodai," the pilot said. "We were going to Kodai."

CHAPTER 8

Qui-Gon thanked the pilot and got to his feet. He had no way of knowing if the ship was really going to Kodai or not; Dr. Lundi was certainly smart enough to throw them off the trail or even deftly set a trap. But they had nothing else to go on. The sooner they could get to Kodai to investigate, the better.

"Do you need help getting somewhere?" Qui-Gon asked the pilot.

The pilot got to his feet. Though it had been only minutes since he'd woken up, he was already quite steady. "No, I'll be fine," he replied. "But if you find my ship, you know where I am."

"Of course," Qui-Gon said. "We'll do what we can."

Obi-Wan and Qui-Gon quickly left the small hangar and made their way down the street and into a larger one. It was full of ships of all sizes, and pilots from all over the galaxy talking shop or tinkering with their vessels. It seemed like it would be easy enough to hire one of them.

Qui-Gon strode up to a pilot and asked if he would take them to Kodai. "Kodai?" the pilot repeated. "You've got the wrong guy."

"I'll take you there, but I won't land — at least not until next week," said another.

Qui-Gon asked half a dozen pilots before he finally found one who was willing to make the journey, a humanoid who wouldn't give them a last name. "Call me Elda," she said before agreeing to drop them off and leave immediately. She could not be convinced to wait around for the return trip.

The Jedi could not afford to be choosy. They boarded right away. While the pilot readied the ship, they settled in for the journey.

"Not many people want to go to Kodai right now," Elda said as she keyed the destination points into her navcomputer.

Qui-Gon raised an eyebrow. "I gathered as much," he said. "Why is that?"

The pilot turned to look over her shoulder at Qui-Gon, giving him an "If you don't know I'm not going to tell you," look.

Qui-Gon didn't prod. *It's just as well*, he thought. *I can get the information from the Temple.*

Stepping out of the cockpit and into the hold,

Qui-Gon switched on his comlink. He had heard of Kodai, and thought it was located somewhere in the Outer Rim Territories. If he was not mistaken, its surface was mostly covered by a vast sea.

His comlink crackled to life and a moment later Temple Archivist Jocasta Nu's voice echoed quietly in the hold of the ship.

"It is good to hear from you, Qui-Gon," she said. "How is the mission going?"

"It's hard to tell at the moment," Qui-Gon responded honestly. "I was hoping you could provide me with information on the planet Kodai."

"Kodai, in the Outer Rim," she said. There was a brief silence as Jocasta plugged the data for the request into her Temple computer. "I seem to remember something about a massive, swelling sea."

Qui-Gon could hear Jocasta pressing buttons and keys on a computer. Then she spoke.

"Kodai is, in fact, covered by a giant sea — a sea that hundreds of years ago swelled so much that it drowned most of the planet's land-dwelling inhabitants," she reported. "Today there is only one pocket of land — a single city. It is sparsely populated by a few thousand Kodaians who spend most of their time trying to preserve their way of life on land, in spite of the fact that most believe that the sea will rage again and kill them all." Jocasta was silent for a moment. Qui-Gon guessed that she was reading ahead.

"Interesting," she murmured. "It seems that the sea has shown no signs of raging in the last hundred years. In fact, the opposite seems to occur. Every ten years, when the planet's two moons sync up, the sea experiences a spectacularly low tide."

"I see," said Qui-Gon, filing away this information.

"That's not all," Jocasta said. "What's particularly fascinating is that the planet's moons will be syncing up the day after tomorrow."

"Interesting timing," Qui-Gon agreed. It seemed obvious enough that Lundi's trip to Kodai at this particular moment and his search for mining equipment were not coincidences. But he was still not clear about why it had been so difficult to find a pilot to take them to Kodai.

Jocasta was quiet for several long moments while Qui-Gon digested this information. When she did not end the transmission, Qui-Gon guessed that she had more to tell him.

"Is there something else?" he finally asked.

"Yes," Jocasta replied slowly. "Another collection of Sith materials was found — this time on the planet Tynna in the Expansion Region. And a strange explosion has occurred on the peaceful planet Nubia. Nobody has come forward to take credit for the blast, but a drawing of a crude Sith Holocron had been scraped onto a duracrete wall outside the ruined building."

Qui-Gon closed his eyes for a moment. The discovery of the additional stash was not surprising. But an explosion was something new — something deadly. The situation was heating up, and he felt a great deal of pressure to defuse it.

"Thank you for the information," Qui-Gon told Jocasta. "We will be in touch if we need anything further."

"Of course, Qui-Gon. I will be here if you need me."

As Jocasta switched off her comlink, Qui-Gon felt a pang of sorrow. He wished that those parting words had been spoken by the woman at the Temple who had helped him with research in the past — Tahl. Qui-Gon had been deeply in love with Tahl, and though she had been killed several months ago, her absence still felt like a blade in his chest.

Qui-Gon put away his comlink and sat down on the floor to meditate until the path was clear. He was just beginning to feel his body relax when Obi-Wan rushed into the hold.

"Master!" he shouted, alarmed. "There's a bomb on board!"

CHAPTER 9

Qui-Gon was on his feet in an instant. He followed his apprentice to the bridge, where the bomb had been planted underneath a low shelf. Bending down carefully, Qui-Gon examined the device. It was black and square with a simple timer on top — and a crude drawing of a Sith Holocron etched into the side.

"I suppose I should have expected something like this," Elda griped from her seat at the controls. "I just hope your famous Jedi powers can defuse that thing before it blows up my ship — and us along with it."

"I'll do my best," Qui-Gon said wryly. "Do you have a set of tools we could use?"

The pilot pointed to a small box in the corner. "You should find everything you need in there," she said.

Obi-Wan brought the tools over to his Master and crouched down beside him. "This symbol is becoming familiar," he noted. "But the device itself does not look too sophisticated."

"It should not be a problem to defuse," Qui-Gon said, casting a glance toward the captain. "But I'm not so sure about our pilot's temper."

Obi-Wan cracked a smile. Leave it to Qui-Gon to find humor in a moment like this.

Qui-Gon opened the tool kit and pulled out a long, slender pick. After carefully inserting it into the side of the bomb casing, he slid it back and forth until he heard an audible beep. The box opened and several strands of colorful wire popped out. A timer behind the wires indicated that the bomb would go off in less than a minute.

"Not much time," Obi-Wan murmured quietly.

Qui-Gon knew his Padawan was right, and he had not expected to see so many different colored wires inside the bomb. It was a more complicated design than he'd originally thought.

Focusing his energy on the bomb, he snipped all of the red wires. But the timer did not switch off. It now read forty seconds, and was counting down.

"Perhaps it is this black wire," Obi-Wan suggested quietly.

Qui-Gon did not think this was likely. It was the only black wire, and too obvious a solution. But as he studied the wire, he sensed that there was indeed something significant about it. Still, he wasn't sure that cutting it was the right thing to do.

"Twenty seconds," Obi-Wan said.

Qui-Gon looked at the bomb more closely. One end of the black wire ran directly into the metal inside the casing. At the other end the black plasticoating ended a few millimeters before the wire touched the metal. Underneath the missing black coating was a series of bright yellow wires. They fanned out to form a row and slid neatly into a metal jack.

"Ten seconds."

Qui-Gon reached down and placed his thumb and forefinger on either side of the yellow wires. Closing his eyes, he twisted them away from the jack. There was a small popping sound as the wires pulled free.

The timer on the bomb continued to count down. But when it reached one second, it suddenly stopped.

"You did it, Master," Obi-Wan said, sounding relieved.

Qui-Gon opened his eyes and saw the number frozen on the timer. "With time to spare," he said wryly.

"I guess you Jedi are good for something," Elda grumped. But there was humor in her voice, and she was smiling broadly. "Thank you," she added quietly.

Qui-Gon put the tools back into the case and got to his feet. "You're welcome," he said.

Back in the hold, Qui-Gon closed his eyes and started to meditate for the second time that day. The planted bomb was something else to consider. Was it meant to kill them, or simply throw them off guard? And who had planted it? It must have been someone who was following them closely, someone who was highly prepared. Not much time had elapsed between the Jedi arranging their travel and their subsequent takeoff.

Qui-Gon began to breathe deeply, letting his mind clear and then focus. But something was interfering with his concentration. His Padawan was pacing.

Qui-Gon opened an eye. "Why don't you try some meditation?" he asked.

Obi-Wan nodded and sat down. Even after he had stopped pacing the room, Qui-Gon could tell he was still agitated. With both eyes open now, he studied his Padawan. Obi-Wan sat cross-legged in a chair with his eyes closed. But his shoulders were tensed, and beneath his eyelids Qui-Gon could see movement.

"Are you all right, Obi-Wan?" Qui-Gon asked softly.

Obi-Wan opened his eyes and met his

Master's gaze. "Yes," he said slowly. And then, "Well, I don't know."

"You are afraid," Qui-Gon stated plainly.

A look of shame came over Obi-Wan's face, but he did not deny it. "My heart is full of dread," he admitted. "I wish we were on another mission — any other mission. I am not sure I have the courage to face the Holocron . . ."

Qui-Gon leaned toward his apprentice. "You have every right to be afraid," he said quietly. "Allow yourself to feel the fear — really feel it — and then let the emotion go. If it comes back, feel it again and let it go again. There should be no shame in one's emotions."

"I am not at fault if it comes back?" Obi-Wan asked, looking up.

"No, Padawan," Qui-Gon replied. "We cannot control how we feel. Only how we choose to handle our feelings."

A look of true relief crossed Obi-Wan's face, and he smiled slightly. His shoulders relaxed and he closed his eyes. Qui-Gon could almost see the fear leaving his Padawan. He was glad his advice had provided some relief.

Sitting back, he closed his eyes, too. He only hoped the advice would work as well for him.

CHAPTER 10

By the time the ship landed on Kodai, Obi-Wan felt refreshed and no longer afraid. He was ready to move forward with the mission. Unfortunately, doing so was not going to be easy.

Although the Jedi were quite certain that they were on the right planet, it was not at all obvious where they should go or what they should do. It was only clear that they were running out of time.

Not to mention that wherever they went, they seemed to be attacked. Their pursuer, or pursuers, would not be shaken and wanted them stopped.

After dropping the Jedi off on a tiny platform in the sole island city of Rena, Elda entered new coordinates into her navcomputer.

"Don't think I'm sticking around just because you diffused that bomb," she grumbled, eyeing the shabby-looking city. "Good luck to both of you," she added, shaking her head. "I have a feeling you're going to need it."

"Thanks for the support," Obi-Wan said dryly as he and Qui-Gon walked down the ship's ramp. "And the transport, of course."

Out in the bright sunshine, the Jedi had to shade their eyes until they adjusted to the light reflecting off the vast sea. The city was small and appeared to have few inhabitants outside. There were cantinas, a single lodging house, and a marketplace where locals exchanged and bought food, most of which was harvested from the sea. Giant walls lined the streets — an attempt at flood protection, Obi-Wan guessed.

While the locals didn't stare at them — in fact, nobody looked at them at all — Obi-Wan got the feeling that they were definitely being noticed. The Kodaians were trying too hard *not* to look at them. As the Jedi approached they cast their yellow eyes downward or bent their slender necks to study the horizon in the opposite direction.

"Do you get the feeling they wish we were invisible?" Qui-Gon asked. "Our presence seems to pain them."

"Exactly," Obi-Wan agreed. It was a strange feeling.

"Let's check the lodging quarters," Qui-Gon

suggested. "We need a place to stay, and Lundi may be there as well."

Obi-Wan nodded in agreement and they strolled into a shabby but clean lobby. A thin Kodaian sat on a stool behind a counter. When he saw the no-longer-disguised Jedi, he nervously got to his feet.

"May I assist you with something?" he asked, fiddling with his stubby fingers and gazing at the floor. Obi-Wan wondered if he was always this agitated around his customers.

"We would like to rent one of your spaces," Qui-Gon explained. "Do you have any to spare?"

The Kodaian closed his golden eyes for a moment, surprised by the question, and Obi-Wan guessed that Kodai and the quarters did not have visitors particularly often. After taking Qui-Gon's credits, the Kodaian placed a card with a door code on the counter. Their room was 4R.

"We are also looking for a Quermian guest we believe you have at the moment. A Doctor Murk Lundi."

The Kodian winced at the mention of Lundi's name. Without making eye contact he pointed to an old turbolift at the end of the hall. "His quarters are on the second floor, number 2F."

The Kodaian looked around to see if anyone was nearby before continuing, then leaned forward and addressed Obi-Wan's boots. "He's a fine guest. He hasn't spoken to anyone since he got here. Hasn't even come out of his room."

Obi-Wan thought this was interesting information. He had gotten the distinct impression that the professor liked an audience. Any audience.

"Thank you," Qui-Gon said, taking the key.

The Jedi made their way down the hall and stepped into the turbolift. An older model, it shuddered as it moved up the single flight to the second floor.

Dr. Lundi's room was located at the end of the hall, and the room next to it was rented out. With the exception of breaking in or listening at the door, there was no way to know what was going on inside.

Obi-Wan put his ear to the door and focused his auditory senses, but found it difficult to concentrate. It almost felt as if something was blocking his connection to the Force. He could not hear anything on the other side.

"Why do you suppose he would hurry to get here only to lock himself up and do nothing?" Obi-Wan asked.

"We do not know what he is doing," Qui-Gon pointed out. "It's impossible to tell what is going on inside."

Another dead end. Obi-Wan let out a long sigh. Fear and frustration began to well in him once again, and he closed his eyes and relaxed his muscles until he felt these emotions fade. It was not easy, but he was able to do it.

Qui-Gon was smiling faintly and nodding at him when Obi-Wan opened his eyes. "Well done, Padawan." He pointed toward the turbolift. "Perhaps we can gather information if we talk to the Kodaians," he added, turning away from the closed door.

Obi-Wan followed. "Right," he said sarcastically. "After we get them to look deep into our eyes."

"So glad to see you are maintaining a sense of humor," Qui-Gon said as they stepped back into the turbolift.

Back outside, it quickly became clear that it would be nearly impossible to get Kodaians to talk to them openly.

"Excuse me," Obi-Wan said, trying to appear friendly as he approached a Kodaian woman.

The Kodaian stopped but did not look up at the Jedi. She stepped from one foot to the other as if unable to stand still. "Yes?" she whispered.

"We are looking for information about a Quermian visitor. A professor. He is here to dig up an artifact at the bottom of the sea —"

At the mention of the bottom of the sea the woman looked up, clearly alarmed. Her eyes were as large as saucers and her hands began to tremble. "I cannot help you," she said. "I must go now."

Watching her hurry away, Obi-Wan wondered if her fear was caused by interaction with outlanders or the mention of the sea, the current state of the moons, and the impending low tide. Or perhaps Kodaians simply lived in a constant state of fear because of their difficult past. Whatever the reason, she clearly did not want to share information.

Obi-Wan was looking around for someone else who might talk to them when he spotted a young boy watching them from several meters away. Unlike the other Kodaians, he looked right at them and did not seem afraid.

"Have you seen a visitor with a long neck and many arms and hands?" Qui-Gon asked, approaching the boy.

The boy nodded and pointed to the lodging quarters. "He's inside. But hasn't come out. If you want information, go to the cantina and ask for Reis. He'll tell you whatever you want to know."

Obi-Wan smiled down at the boy, grateful for the tip. "Thanks," he said.

Reis was not hard to find. He sat in a bare, dingy corner sipping a mug of drale, the only humanoid in the place. His gray hair was matted against his head and his face was unshaven.

But his dark eyes were sharp as he took in the approaching Jedi.

"Mind if we sit down?" Qui-Gon asked.

Reis continued to size up each of the Jedi in turn, pausing where their lightsabers hung from their utility belts. "Not at all," he said. "I've always got time to talk to Jedi. Suppose you want to know all about the Holocron, eh?"

Obi-Wan felt a wave of shock at the mention of the word *Holocron*. Finally, someone else said it first. Perhaps now they would get the answers they so desperately needed.

The Jedi were quick to sit down, and Reis smiled. "Thought that might get your attention," he said. He took a long swig of drale.

"It's there, all right," he said, putting the mug down. "Been there for thousands of years. Problem is, no one can seem to get it. Everyone wants it, but no one can get it. They try, but turn up dead or crazy every time."

"Yet attempts are still made to retrieve it?" Qui-Gon asked.

"Of course. People can't leave that kind of power alone," Reis replied with a wave of his grubby hand. He leaned toward the Jedi, and Obi-Wan could smell the stale drale on his breath. "I've heard that somebody, somewhere has offered to pay an incredibly large fortune for the Holocron. Nobody knows who it is. Still, it makes going after it a pretty desirable propo —"

Obi-Wan suddenly stopped listening when a familiar figure entered the bar. It looked like Omal, from Dr. Lundi's lecture on Coruscant. The younger Jedi squinted, but the cantina was dark and he couldn't be sure. With a pang of guilt he realized that his observation abilities hadn't been their strongest at the lecture. Things had been a little hazy.

"Excuse me," Obi-Wan said, getting up from his chair and ignoring Qui-Gon's quizzical look. If it was Omal, Obi-Wan wanted to talk to him.

Obi-Wan crossed the cantina quickly, but not quickly enough. Whoever was at the bar saw him coming. With a panicked glance over his shoulder, the person disappeared out the door and into the street.

CHAPTER 11

Obi-Wan rolled over on his sleep couch for the hundredth time. He could not rest. He wasn't sure if the synchronizing moons were the cause of his restlessness, or if it was just the ominous feeling he hadn't been able to shake since he first encountered Murk Lundi. Either way, he could not sleep.

Giving up entirely, Obi-Wan left the lodging quarters and wandered down to the beach. Perhaps the rhythmic sound of the waves would soothe him. He needed to get some rest before taking a turn watching Lundi's door. Qui-Gon's shift was nearly up.

Obi-Wan's steps echoed in the still night as he walked. The darkness seemed to swallow him. After donning his night goggles he walked and walked, expecting to see and hear the water at any moment.

I'm sure the sea was much closer to the main

street than this, he thought. Obi-Wan suddenly felt confused, as if he had walked onto a completely different planet. Wasn't Kodai covered by a vast sea?

Obi-Wan stopped and stared ahead, concentrating hard. At first he could not see any water. Then he thought he saw a liquid shimmer, but it was far away. He suddenly realized that the water had receded hundreds of kilometers since that afternoon.

Peering in the other direction, he spotted a large group of Kodaians farther down the beach. They carried torches and hovered around what appeared to be an ancient ruined structure, frantically digging at the seafloor. They were obviously trying to scavenge parts of the city that were lost in the flood hundreds of years ago.

Watching them from a distance, Obi-Wan was suddenly filled with a deep sense of sadness. It would be awful to lose so much of your history to a raging sea. And to be tortured every ten years by the opportunity to find the broken pieces of it.

Obi-Wan turned back to the water — or lack of it. In the near darkness he could not even be sure that the reflections he saw were, in fact, the sea.

An image and a voice flashed in Obi-Wan's head — Lundi storming out of the storehouse on Nolar. "I just have to time it right," he had said.

With a jolt, Obi-Wan knew that Lundi had been waiting for the water to recede so that he could get the Holocron. The Kodaian sea would be at its lowest tide in a decade in just over an hour.

Obi-Wan raced through the darkness back to the lodging quarters. Outside the building he spotted someone racing away. Omal? Unfortunately it was too dark to tell, and he had no time to go after the figure. He had to get to Qui-Gon. When his comlink wouldn't go through, he headed back.

"Master!" Obi-Wan shouted, but stopped short. Qui-Gon was not at his lookout post and the door to the professor's room was wide open. No one was inside.

Suddenly Qui-Gon was behind him assessing the situation. "I was only gone a moment," he breathed. "I got a communication from Jocasta Nu and stepped away. He can't be far."

Once again Obi-Wan felt frustration well inside him. How were they going to locate Lundi and the Holocron now?

"We'll have to go on our instincts," Qui-Gon

said, as if reading his Padawan's mind. "If we listen carefully the Force will guide us."

Obi-Wan knew his Master was right. And anyway, they had no other choice.

Silently, Obi-Wan led Qui-Gon toward the water. The seemingly endless beach was now teeming with Kodaians and their digging tools. Pausing for a moment to close his eyes and focus, Obi-Wan sensed that there was a deserted area farther north on the sand.

The Jedi walked out for several kilometers, moving as quickly as they could. All around them Kodaians were uncovering artifacts from the infamous flood. Some held their newly discovered treasures high above their heads with glee, while others fell to their knees in tears. Obi-Wan felt for them.

Up ahead was a strangely deserted strip of sodden land. Kodaians worked busily on either side of it, but the raised area was completely empty.

"It's almost as if an invisible barrier is keeping them away from this area," Obi-Wan commented.

"Perhaps one is," Qui-Gon replied, looking around.

The Jedi hurried ahead. Several Kodaians stopped their digging and stared after them.

They did not avert their eyes now. Some even shouted warnings. The Jedi ignored them. As Obi-Wan moved forward, he began to feel something dark and powerful surrounding him. Horror and relief collided within him. They were definitely approaching the right place. The Sith Holocron was not far away.

Letting his fear slip through him like water through a sieve, Obi-Wan moved forward. He was so intent on finding Lundi and the Holocron that he didn't see the crevasse in front of him.

"Obi-Wan, stop!" Qui-Gon shouted from behind.

Obi-Wan skidded to a halt centimeters before a yawning black chasm. He peered into it, but could see nothing but darkness. A wave of evil energy wafted up at him. *The Holocron.*

Without speaking, the Jedi pulled out their cable launchers and anchored the ends firmly into the seafloor next to the crevasse. A thousand thoughts were running through Obi-Wan's mind, and he wanted to express them all to his Master. But doing so was impossible.

Glancing at each other only briefly, Qui-Gon and Obi-Wan simultaneously rappelled over the edge into the blackness. Before long the top of the cliff disappeared from view.

The crevasse wall was slippery and wet. Obi-

Wan took a deep breath as he continued to descend. Part of him wanted to know what he would find below, and part of him didn't.

Suddenly he felt a flicker of movement in his cable. A second later his anchor flew over the edge, and Obi-Wan found himself careening into the darkness below.

CHAPTER 12

Qui-Gon saw a figure standing above them at the top of the chasm. It leaned over the edge for a split second, then was gone. A moment later Obi-Wan's launcher cord went slack and his Padawan fell past him with alarming speed.

Qui-Gon immediately anchored himself to the cliff and reached out to the Force to try and stop the fall. But the dark energy in the giant crevasse worked against him. He felt oddly exhausted and had little ability to concentrate.

Quickly, Qui-Gon pushed past his weakness and focused harder. He willed his apprentice to do the same.

The sound of Obi-Wan's launcher anchor scraping against the side of the crevasse was music to Qui-Gon's ears. After a few seemingly endless seconds it caught, jerking Obi-Wan to an abrupt halt. He dangled in the air somewhere below Qui-Gon.

"Are you all right, Obi-Wan?" Qui-Gon called down. His voice echoed off the chasm walls.

"I'm fine," Obi-Wan replied. "And I can see the bottom of the crevasse."

Qui-Gon tested his line. It was still secure. Then he rappelled the rest of the way as quickly as he could. By the time he got to the crevasse floor, Obi-Wan had stowed his cable launcher and was searching the area by the light of a glow rod. The crevasse floor was rocky and covered by slippery vegetation. They would have to tread carefully.

"I don't see anything," Obi-Wan said. His voice sounded strangely hollow, and Qui-Gon wasn't sure if it was because of the chasm, his fall, or because they were so close to the Holocron. The concentration of dark knowledge could tap one's strength. He certainly felt a bit weakened himself. But the strange hollow feeling also let Qui-Gon know they were on the right track. He felt at once repelled and drawn closer.

Qui-Gon ignited a second glow rod and the Jedi searched the area until they came across a series of footprints. With the wet vegetation covering the chasm floor, it was impossible to tell if there was more than one set of marks.

As they moved farther away from their decension point, Qui-Gon heard a low rumble. It sounded as though a storm was picking up. Or was the sea rising? It was now well past the time of the lowest tide and the water should be coming back up.

A flash of lightning split the sky above. In the blast of light, Qui-Gon thought he saw a figure struggling toward them. But before he could be certain, a plume of water began to gush up through a large gap in the rocky shelf they were standing on. Shooting meters above his head, it completely blocked Qui-Gon's view and nearly knocked both Jedi off their feet. As it rained down on them and seeped into his boots, Qui-Gon was surprised to find that the water was hot.

With a sudden sense of dread Qui-Gon realized that they were at the bottom of one crevasse, but that there were probably several just like it below. The seafloor was a honeycomb. They were by no means on solid ground.

Water continued to push out of the hole with remarkable force. There was no question that the tide was turning. When the gush finally subsided, they were up to their ankles in hot seawater. Several meters ahead of him, on the other side of the gap, Qui-Gon could see a crumpled form lying on the crevasse floor.

Qui-Gon ran blindly toward the figure. Was it Murk Lundi?

It was. The Quermian lay limply on the crevasse floor with his face partially in the water. The apparatus that normally covered one of his eyes was gone, revealing an empty socket.

Qui-Gon was almost upon the professor when he lashed out. "You can't stop me!" he cried, lifting his head. One of his gangly arms fumbled for something under his robe, and he shakily pulled out a blaster. The weapon wobbled in his hand, and he fired recklessly.

Qui-Gon quickly dodged, escaping the blast in spite of the close range. Behind him, Obi-Wan ignited his lightsaber. The blue blade cut through the air, deflecting the bolt and knocking Lundi's blaster out of his hand. The weapon skittered across the crevasse floor and fell into the geyser gap.

"No!" Lundi cried. He struggled to get to his feet, then collapsed in the water.

"Where is the Holocron?" Obi-Wan demanded, pulling the Quermian to his feet.

"In my hand! In my hand! I held it in my hand!" Lundi screeched, jabbing at Obi-Wan with his pointed fingers.

"Where is it now?" Obi-Wan asked through gritted teeth, binding as many of the professor's skinny wrists together as he could catch.

"Let me go. Let me get it. It's not for you!" Lundi spat in Obi-Wan's face and flailed wildly but he did not have the strength to break free. "I should be the one!"

Qui-Gon's mind reeled. He could feel that they were close to the Holocron. Very close. He tried to focus, to find its location, but the dark side was playing tricks with his mind. It was so near and still beyond his mental vision. There was so much he didn't understand. If Lundi had held the Holocron, where was it now? Did someone else have it? Had he been unable to handle the power?

Questions were still forming in his mind when the rock beneath Qui-Gon's feet shuddered. For a split second the Jedi Master considered diving into the swirling waters to find his answers. With a glance at his apprentice his sanity returned. If the Jedi could not recover the Holocron it was unlikely that anyone else could, either.

"I'll carry him," Qui-Gon told his Padawan abruptly. He did not want to waste his strength explaining himself.

Before Qui-Gon could lift Lundi from the chasm floor, a second rush of water hurtled out of the gap. Obi-Wan saw it coming and steadied his Master, helping him get the Quermian onto a shoulder. But now the water was halfway up their calves.

Obi-Wan led the way, holding his glow rod

out in front of them. They had to walk carefully along the rocky shelf, back to the crevasse wall. The water around Qui-Gon's legs made it difficult to know where to step, and Lundi was continuously flailing several arms and raving in his ear.

"The Holocron!" he screamed, struggling against Qui-Gon's firm grip. "I must get the Holocron! It's mine. Mine!"

Qui-Gon tried to ignore the professor, which wasn't easy. Finally he could see the place where they'd descended. But how were they going to get back up to the top with a maddened Quermian and only one anchored cable launcher?

"I can climb up and toss the cable back down to you," Obi-Wan suggested.

Qui-Gon wasn't sure they had time for that — or that he could make it while holding onto Lundi. But he didn't see a better option, and he couldn't think with Lundi screaming in his ear.

Obi-Wan had just hoisted himself off the rocky shelf when a small ship appeared overhead. Dropping back to the floor, he and his encumbered Master pressed themselves against the crevasse wall for cover. There was no way of knowing who was inside, or what they were after.

The ship descended as close to the crevasse

as it could, and a long ladder dropped down in front of the Jedi. The vessel looked vaguely familiar, but in the darkness it was hard to identify it. Obi-Wan looked at his Master with uncertainty. Qui-Gon was not clear about the ship, either. But he was not one to refuse help that they truly needed.

The Jedi grabbed hold and climbed. Even with the evenly spaced rungs, getting the struggling professor safely to the ship was no easy feat. About halfway up, Lundi passed out. When Qui-Gon finally pulled himself into the ship, he was exhausted. Holding Lundi with one arm Qui-Gon gripped each step with his teeth in order to move his free hand to the next step. Twice his boots slipped on the wet rungs, nearly sending him and his heavy load into the waters below. At last he reached the ship's hatch and dragged himself and his burden aboard.

"Nice to see you again," came a gritty female voice from the cockpit. Qui-Gon was surprised to see Elda. She grinned at his reaction.

"Didn't expect to see me, did you?" she asked.

Qui-Gon shook his head. "But it's a pleasure," he told her sincerely. "Thank you for coming."

The pilot turned back to her controls and lifted the ship into the air. "You don't have to thank me," she replied. "Something about you or this place got under my skin, and I came back shortly after leaving. I just couldn't leave you here. After all, you saved my ship from being blown up. I wanted to return the favor."

"We're grateful," Obi-Wan remarked as he slumped into a chair.

Qui-Gon set Lundi down in another seat and secured him to it with a length of cable. He didn't think the old Quermian would have much strength when he woke, but he didn't want to take any chances.

Suddenly the professor's head snapped up.

Qui-Gon stepped back, but Lundi craned his long neck forward, forcing the Jedi against the ship wall.

The Quermian's good eye rolled around in its socket as he closely examined the Jedi. "Peace-makers!" he spat. "You have begun a war." Lundi whipped his small head back and forth on the end of his slender neck. "War! War!" he repeated over and over, each time his voice growing louder and more shrill.

Qui-Gon opened his mouth to speak but saw that it would be of little use. He could only watch as the once brilliant historian whipped himself into a frenzy. The power of the dark side had corrupted him. It was clear to the Jedi Master that Lundi was insane. He would be escorted back to the Temple and evaluated. Qui-

Gon felt quite certain that he would need psychiatric help. And there were also questions for the Galactic Republic regarding what he'd intended to *do* with the Holocron.

This was not the way Qui-Gon had hoped to return from this mission. He did not have the Holocron. His apprentice seemed rattled. There was also still the question of who, besides the Jedi and Professor Lundi, knew it was down there. Who had unfastened Obi-Wan's cable launcher? Had anyone else been able to get down into the chasm? The best they could hope for was that the Holocron was still at the bottom of Kodaian sea — at least until the tide dropped again in ten years.

"You can't handle it! You don't know what to do with it! You don't deserve it!" The professor raved on. Qui-Gon wasn't sure if Lundi was even talking to him any longer.

Taking a deep breath, Qui-Gon tuned out Lundi's mad rants. He tried to quiet his mind, consoling himself with the fact that the Holocron was not in Lundi's possession. Still, he knew this mission was far from over.

Ten Years Later

CHAPTER 13

"Pathetic weaklings," Lundi spat. His uncovered eye rolled in its socket and a line of drool dribbled down his chin. "The power was mine — within my grasp. But you . . . you snatched it. You stole it away."

Obi-Wan watched the insane Quermian struggle in his bindings. The anger seething inside him was tangible, and the Jedi felt certain that Lundi would kill him if he could. But aside from the lucid declaration of the power he'd nearly had and then lost, much of what the professor said was incomprehensible.

Professor Lundi had almost lost his life on Kodai when he'd attempted to go after the Sith Holocron buried under the planet's vast sea. He'd survived, but his sanity was gone — eaten away by the ancient device lurking under the pounding waves.

Lundi writhed in his seat, trying to get free.

Since that fateful night on Kodai he'd been tried for the crime of attempting to bring a great evil into active existence in the galaxy. Not only was he trying to obtain the Holocron, there was significant evidence that he'd intended to use it for evil purposes.

This was not a crime the Republic took lightly.

Lundi himself had confessed to the crime. In fact, during the trial he'd boasted about momentarily having the Holocron in his hands. It wasn't easy to get his statement. His rants sometimes lasted days, ending only when the mad Quermian collapsed. Even then, after he'd been bound and put in a cell so that he couldn't hurt himself — or anyone else — he continued to twitch and mutter angrily in his sleep.

"Weak child," Lundi growled, glaring at Obi-Wan through the bars of his cell. "You are nothing. Nothing."

Obi-Wan stared back at the professor. His feelings for Murk Lundi had not changed in ten years. The professor's evil and insanity thoroughly repulsed him, and Obi-Wan would have liked to remain as far from Lundi as possible. But he could not defy the Council's decision. An assignment was an assignment.

Obi-Wan had been surprised when he and his Padawan, Anakin Skywalker, were summoned to the Temple earlier that day. Out of the blue,

the mission they were on was taken over by another Jedi team. This had never happened to
Obi-Wan before. Whenever he and his deceased Master Qui-Gon Jinn or he and Anakin
were assigned to a mission, they always saw it
through to completion. At least until now.

As they'd made their way through the Temple
corridors, Obi-Wan had noted that Anakin
was annoyed by the abrupt shift in plans. The
thirteen-year-old apprentice had clearly been
enjoying himself on the originally assigned
mission — it allowed him to tinker with the
weapons systems on a sleek ship.

"This better be good," he'd grumped.

Obi-Wan had counseled the boy, telling him
that even if it wasn't "good," it would certainly
be important. Anakin had merely rolled his eyes
as they'd entered the Jedi Council Chambers.

Obi-Wan had momentarily marveled at this.
As a Padawan learner, entering the Council
Chambers always made his palms sweat, his
heart race. An incredibly important place to be,
it never failed to make him slightly nervous.
Anakin never showed signs of nervousness
upon entering the Council Chambers. He simply
walked right in, as if it were the home of an old
friend.

As soon as he and Anakin had entered the
Chambers, Obi-Wan knew that whatever had

brought them there was serious. All of the Jedi Masters were present, and the expression on Yoda's face was unusually grave.

"Rumblings once again about the Sith Holocron on Kodai there are," Yoda said, not wasting any time. "Planning to recover it someone is."

Obi-Wan had felt a wave of fear go through him. He'd been having troubling dreams and visions for several nights. At first he hadn't been sure why. Then he'd realized that almost exactly ten years had passed since he and Qui-Gon had first followed Dr. Murk Lundi to the Sith Holocron. The moons of Kodai would soon be in synchronous orbit, once again causing an amazingly low tide. And that was when attempts were made to recover the Holocron.

"That is not all," Master Ki-Adi Mundi added. There was a moment of silence in the Chambers before he went on.

"Jedi all over the galaxy have been receiving threatening messages about the Sith gaining power. Some of these messages contain images of Jedi being brutally killed."

Mace Windu cleared his throat. "At first we believed these threats to be the work of trivial criminals out for attention," he said. "But given the dangerous nature of the information in the Holocron and the fact that the Sith have returned, we must treat these threats very seriously."

"Take action immediately, we must," Master Yoda said, nodding slightly. "Fall into the wrong hands, the Holocron must not. Give the Sith such a victory, we *must not*."

Standing before the semicircle of Jedi Masters, Obi-Wan had briefly closed his eyes. He could feel his body filling with dread and wanted to let it wash through him. Doing so had not been easy.

Obi-Wan knew that he and Anakin were the obvious Jedi team for this mission. After all, he was more familiar with Lundi, the Holocron, and Kodai than any other living Jedi. But it was not an assignment he looked forward to — or even felt comfortable with. Not only was he without the help and guidance of Qui-Gon, but his Master had died at the hand of an emergent Sith Lord.

"What's the matter, Jedi?" Lundi spat. "Lost in a memory?"

Obi-Wan was jolted back to the moment. Something wet splattered across his face. Lundi's saliva.

"You'd better wat —" Anakin started to shout protectively. But Obi-Wan quickly raised an arm to quiet his Padawan.

Calmly wiping his face with the sleeve of his

robe, Obi-Wan gazed back at the professor. He would not show anger or frustration. Though he desperately wished he could go on this mission without this crazed, evil being, he knew he could not. Their best chance of stopping anyone seeking the Holocron was to have Lundi's wealth of knowledge — however garbled and menacing — with them.

Obi-Wan stared into the old Quermian's visible eye, searching for a glimmer of repentance or sanity. Either one would grant him a small sense of hope.

But as Murk Lundi glared back at him, Obi-Wan saw neither.

CHAPTER 14

Anakin took a small step forward, trying to see into the Quermian's eye. It was a difficult task, since his head bobbed and weaved like a bird's. Anakin knew this to be a symptom of insanity. As a boy on Tatooine, he'd seen some of the street dwellers do the same thing.

But this was different. Standing in front of Lundi's cell in the mental hospital, Anakin felt intrigued. There was something strong here — something powerful.

Anakin noted how Lundi's uncovered eye narrowed to a dark slit as he glared at Obi-Wan. It burned with a fiery hatred. He'd never seen anyone look at Obi-Wan like that. It was a little unsettling. Of course, Anakin would have chosen unsettling and interesting over boring any day. Today someone had chosen it for him.

Suddenly Lundi lunged forward, thrusting his

head and long Quermian neck between the bars. Anakin leaned back as Lundi began to rant about the Holocron yet again.

"Moons are moving. Tides are turning," he rambled. A few of his gangly arms waved in the air. "I knew you would not stay away. None have. They all come to me. Crying. Begging. Screaming. 'Teach me, professor. Show me the way.' They think I have failed. But we know different, don't we?" He stared Obi-Wan down, then went on, almost as if he were talking to himself. "Yes, of course we know different. We know I did not fail. I could not fail. I held the power. In my hands I held the power. That is different from failure. But then I was robbed! Robbed by robed thieves on a mission of peace. Here, Jedi. Have a piece of this!"

Lundi's many shackled arms awkwardly thrust his food out of his cell, striking Obi-Wan in the face.

Anakin looked at his Master, expecting to see some sort of reaction. But Obi-Wan didn't flinch. He simply stood before Lundi's cell with a stoic calm.

"We need your help, professor," he said quietly, "to recover the Holocron."

Professor Lundi looked up, clearly surprised. His eye widened and a smile stretched across his face, revealing two rows of decaying teeth. He put his face up to the bars again, and Anakin could smell his rancid breath.

"At last you Jedi have found the right path," he cackled.

CHAPTER 15

It did not take long for Obi-Wan to arrange to have Lundi released into his custody. Obi-Wan, Anakin, and the professor were on a ship bound for Kodai by late afternoon.

Once they had settled in, Obi-Wan tried again to talk to Lundi. Though the Jedi knew the Holocron had last been seen on Kodai, they were not sure if it was still there. And Obi-Wan felt certain that Lundi had additional information that would prove vital to finding the ancient artifact. Even if Lundi did not intend to help the Jedi, it was possible that there would exist unintentional clues in his torrent of words and abuse.

Though he was hardly joyful, Lundi seemed glad to be out of solitary confinement. Rocking back and forth in his restraining cage, he gazed around the hold of the ship like a curious child.

Obi-Wan hoped the change of scenery would help make Lundi more cooperative. He also hoped that the Quermian was lucid enough to provide accurate information.

"The Jedi are not interested in using the Holocron to promote evil," he said, facing Lundi directly. "Rather, we wish to have it recovered so that it can be permanently housed in a safe place."

Lundi's eye glinted, and then he laughed. "You are nothing but a scared weakling — a cowardly boy," he cackled. "You haven't changed at all, and neither have the Jedi. I should have known that the Jedi would not want to tame the Holocron. They do not even have the strength to try."

Out of the corner of his eye, Obi-Wan saw Anakin leap to his feet. "Do not insult my Master!" he shouted. "He knows courage far better than you."

"It is all right, Anakin," Obi-Wan said calmly, placing a reassuring hand on his Padawan's shoulder. "I am not vulnerable to insults."

Obi-Wan watched Anakin turn away and sit down in the copilot's seat. Next to him, the pilot was nervously fiddling with the ship's controls. He was obviously agitated by the professor's ravings. But Lundi was now uncharacteristically silent. Glaring at the Jedi from behind durasteel bars, he did not say a word.

Obi-Wan fitfully rolled over on his sleep couch. It had been more than a day since they'd boarded the ship, and nearly as long since Lundi had spoken. Obi-Wan was now almost certain that Lundi knew who was after the Holocron — and how to get to it before they did. But the Jedi's attempts to pry information out of the professor had proved fruitless. He was locked in a battle of wills with a deranged lunatic, and the deranged lunatic had the upper hand.

Obi-Wan closed his eyes and willed himself to relax. Across the room Anakin was sound asleep, the rhythm of his breathing echoing softly in the small space. Obi-Wan cleared his mind. If he didn't get some rest he would be at a disadvantage when they arrived on Kodai.

Just as he was drifting off, a familiar voice came into Obi-Wan's head.

There were others, Padawan, it said. Obi-Wan let out a long breath. The voice was Qui-Gon's. His deceased Master had always been there to help him, and still was — even in death.

Others were involved in Lundi's search for the Holocron. Contact them. Perhaps Lundi told them something that would be of help to you now.

Obi-Wan opened his eyes. *Thank you, Master,* he thought as he sat up. Getting to his feet, he quietly left the room. He wanted to contact Jocasta Nu as soon as possible. They had a couple of days before the low tide on Kodai. There was no time to lose.

It did not take Jocasta long to locate two of the three students who had been closest to Lundi. Both Omal and Dedra were living on the same planet. Obi-Wan directed the pilot to change course. They reached Omal's apartment the next day.

"Omal was one of Dr. Lundi's brightest students," Obi-Wan explained to Anakin after they made sure Lundi was secure and headed down various streets and alleys. "One of the most devoted followers. I'm hopeful he can give us information we can use to move forward."

The two Jedi walked up a flight of rickety steps to a dingy-looking door. Before knocking Obi-Wan looked around and made mental note of the quickest retreat. Lundi's fame had diminished but there was no guarantee that his former followers would be friendly toward Jedi.

When Omal opened the door, Obi-Wan knew immediately that he was no threat nor would he be able to help them. His clothing was dirty and disheveled. His shoulders drooped, and his eyes were constantly darting about, as if looking at any one thing for too long was incredibly painful. But most of all, it appeared as if Omal's mind was nearly as scrambled as Lundi's. Obi-Wan could almost feel his thoughts bouncing around in his head, bumping into one another and tangling themselves up in knots.

"What do you want?" Omal asked. He glanced at the Jedi's robes, and his hands began to shake.

Sadness and dread washed over Obi-Wan. What had happened to the bright-eyed boy he'd seen at Dr. Lundi's lecture ten years before? What had Lundi — and possibly the Sith Holocron — done to him? And what did that mean to the mission?

"We just want to talk with you, Omal," Obi-Wan said softly. "May we come in?"

Omal didn't reply, but turned away from the door. He meandered into a small living room, and the Jedi followed. Garbage was strewn across the floor and the furniture looked as if it would collapse at any moment. The air was stale and rank. Anakin briefly waved a hand in front of his nose, but Obi-Wan shot him a look that made the boy drop both hands to his sides.

Obi-Wan quickly took in his surroundings,

then turned toward Omal, who was standing awkwardly in the middle of the filthy room. He would have to be gentle with him.

"We are Jedi on an important mission," he began. "We are trying to recover the Sith Holocron so that it can be kept safely. Did Professor Lundi ever mention the artifact to you?"

At the mention of the Holocron Omal began to moan softly, rocking back and forth on his heels. Obi-Wan was about to ask something else when the front door opened and Dedra — the second student of Lundi's — came in with a bag of groceries.

Obi-Wan was relieved to see that for the most part Dedra looked like herself. She was older and had a tired look in her eyes, but had retained her sanity. Resting the bag of food on her hip, she gestured to Obi-Wan for the Jedi to come into the kitchen.

"We'll be right back," Obi-Wan said, excusing himself and Anakin. The two Jedi followed Dedra into the kitchen.

"I am Obi-Wan Kenobi," Obi-Wan said, "and this is my Padawan, Anakin Skywalker." Though he had seen Dedra at a lecture of Professor Lundi's, they had never actually been introduced.

"Your name is not important," Dedra replied.

"I know that you are a Jedi, and suspect that you are looking for the Sith Holocron."

Obi-Wan nodded. "We wish to put it safely away — for good," he explained.

A look of sadness spread across Dedra's face. "That would be nice," she said. "It has already done so much damage to so many." She glanced toward the living room. Obi-Wan knew she was not talking about the ancient tyranny of the Sith.

"Omal's mental state is fragile," she explained. "It is best not to mention Lundi or the Holocron in his presence."

"I gathered that," Obi-Wan said, feeling a twinge of guilt. "Do you know what happened?"

Dedra turned away and began to unpack some of the groceries. It looked as though she was going to feed Omal a meal. "I only know that he hasn't been the same since Professor Lundi's sabbatical ten years ago," she said.

Dedra pulled some vegetables out of a bag and began to wash them. Obi-Wan noticed that her hands were shaking slightly, and she kept her eyes on what she was doing.

"And that is *all* you know?" Obi-Wan asked, looking at her pointedly.

Dedra sighed and her hands dropped into the water basin. "No, not all," she admitted.

Obi-Wan waited patiently for Dedra to continue.

"Ten years ago Omal followed Norval, another of Professor Lundi's star pupils, to Kodai. Norval was fixated on the Holocron, and had secretly joined one of the sects obsessed with obtaining it. He figured out that Lundi was going after it, and decided the professor needed his help. Omal wanted to stop Norval from interfering with Dr. Lundi's attempt. He thought that the kind of power Lundi was talking about would be too much for Norval to handle."

Dedra switched off the water and turned toward Obi-Wan. "I don't know what happened, but it was obviously too much for Omal, too," she said in a whisper. "And since Professor Lundi has been institutionalized ever since, I guess it was too much for him, too."

Obi-Wan was quiet for a moment, thinking. "What happened to Norval?" he finally asked.

A tortured look came into Dedra's eyes. "I don't know," she said mournfully. "But the best I can hope for is that he is dead."

CHAPTER 16

Anakin's eyes widened. That was a terrible thing to say. Even when he was a slave as a young boy on Tatooine, he never wished that his life would end. Death seemed so permanent, so final.

"We didn't know then that Norval had been obsessively studying Dr. Lundi's texts," Dedra explained quickly, seeing the reactions of the Jedi. "He'd developed a taste for power, and he desperately wanted it. The teachings had changed him."

Anakin wasn't sure he understood what Dedra meant. He knew what it was like to want something badly. He'd wanted to win a Podrace on Tatooine. He wanted to free his mother. He wanted to become a Jedi. But he didn't think these desires actually changed him. They were simply part of who he was.

Nobody said anything for several moments.

Anakin sensed that his Master was taking everything in, trying to put all the information in place in his mind.

Suddenly the silence in the kitchen was broken by the sound of Omal's voice. He was mumbling something in the other room. His words were not clear, but the tone was desperate. A look of concern crossed Dedra's face and she moved toward the living room.

"I'll go check on him," Anakin offered. He left Obi-Wan and Dedra in the small kitchen and headed back into the living room. Omal was still sitting on the floor, but his head was now sharply tilted to the side. Tears were running down the side of his face, and his nose was watery.

Anakin stared at Omal for a long moment. He felt sorry for him, and wished there was something he could do to help him. If what his Master said was true, Omal had been horribly and permanently changed.

"You're okay," Anakin said gently, snapping out of his thoughts. "We just need to get your face cleaned up." He found a small scrap of relatively clean cloth and used it to wipe Omal's face. Omal looked up at him gratefully for a brief moment. Then his eyes darted away again and he resumed rocking back and forth.

Anakin watched Omal for what seemed like

an eternity. When he finally looked away, he felt a strong desire to move ahead with the mission. He had to know what had caused Omal's downfall — what had the Jedi Council so up in arms.

He wanted to do it now — to get out of the apartment, get going. Dedra had told them everything she knew, and Omal was clearly not going to tell them anything at all. What was Obi-Wan still doing in the kitchen? Was there a reason it was taking him so long?

Feeling antsy, Anakin began to look around the living room. Piles of dirty clothes, scraps of food, and all kinds of other items were littered across the floor. None of them looked particularly interesting or important.

Then, out of the corner of his eye, Anakin spotted something shiny sticking out from under a tunic. Picking it up, he saw that it was a small holoprojector. Anakin tried to switch it on, but knew almost immediately that it was broken.

From his spot on the floor, Omal began to moan softly. "No, Norval. No," he repeated.

Anakin barely heard him. He loved mechanical things, and couldn't resist tinkering a tiny bit with the projector. He pulled a tool from his utility belt and started to fiddle. But the projector was jammed.

"Blast!" Anakin exclaimed. He was surprised

by his own frustration. He usually loved this kind of challenge.

Anakin was about to toss the faulty projector aside when he pressed the right sequence and it suddenly came to life. At first the image was fuzzy, and Anakin had a hard time making it out. Then, as he began to realize what he was looking at, his mouth gaped open.

It was an image of a Jedi Knight being brutally murdered.

Anakin stood frozen, staring at the image. Behind him, Omal's moaning was getting louder. Finally the sound got through to Anakin, and he tried to switch the projector off. Only now it was jammed on and didn't shut down.

The murder played again, and again. The Ithorian Jedi raised his lightsaber — but was hit from behind by a bolt from a blaster. The Jedi crumpled to the ground, dead.

Anakin's heart began to race. He tried not to look at the image, but something seemed to be holding his eyes to it. And something about what he was looking at felt familiar. It was as if he had seen it before and knew it, somehow. Anakin began to feel ill.

Anakin forced his repair tool into the bottom of the projector and the image disappeared. He tossed the machine back onto the floor and turned away. His hands shook slightly and his knees felt wobbly. Omal's moans gave voice to what Anakin was feeling.

Anakin took a deep breath and tried to clear his head. He knew messages of this sort were being sent around the galaxy, of course. He'd been at the briefing with the Jedi Council and had been told all about them. But he hadn't actually expected to see one. He wasn't prepared.

And now that awful image had been implanted in his mind. Anakin looked over at Omal. He stopped moaning, but his eyes darted back and forth between Anakin and the broken holoprojector on the floor.

Anakin was about to approach him when Obi-Wan came rushing into the living room with Dedra behind him. "I just got a call from the ship," he said. "It seems Dr. Lundi has decided to talk again. And the pilot thinks there are vandals lurking around the hangar. He's threatening to leave Lundi and take off."

Anakin felt relief wash through him and realized just how unsettled he was by Omal's apartment and the projector's message. He wanted to get out of there, and right that second was none too soon.

"Did you tell him to hold tight?" Anakin asked, gratefully following Obi-Wan to the door.

Obi-Wan nodded. "But I'm not sure how long

he'll wait for us. He's been a little jittery since we left Coruscant."

"You can say that again," Anakin said. "The guy has no backbone."

The Jedi said good-bye to Omal and Dedra and hurried back to the ship. Anakin knew that he should tell his Master about the projector and the message, but for some reason didn't want to. It was strange, but he felt guilty about it. It was as if he were somehow responsible for the message, for what happened in it.

But that makes no sense at all, Anakin thought. *I don't even know who those people are. Or were.*

Hurrying after his Master, Anakin decided not to say anything. Obi-Wan seemed distracted, and it wasn't as if the existence of the message was new information. He would tell him later, when the time was right.

CHAPTER 17

"I'll check out the exterior of the ship to make sure there hasn't been any sabotage," Anakin said once they were inside the hangar.

Obi-Wan smiled. He knew his Padawan would rather investigate something mechanical than do just about anything else.

"Okay," he said. "I'll head inside and talk to the captain — and Lundi."

Obi-Wan hurried up the ship's ramp and into the cockpit.

"It's about time," the pilot said, though Obi-Wan thought he seemed relieved to see him. "He's been rambling for the last half hour." He pointed nervously to the hold, where Lundi sat in his cage. "Something about an ancient device that's calling to him. And the tides."

"Thanks," Obi-Wan said, turning toward the hold. He took a deep breath. He wanted this conversation — if that was what it would be — to go well. He *needed* it to go well.

"I've just been to see Dedra and Omal," Obi-Wan said calmly. He watched Lundi closely for some sort of reaction to the names, but didn't see one. Lundi simply glared at him through the dark slit that was his visible eye.

Disappointed, Obi-Wan pushed on. "They had some interesting things to say about Norval."

This time Obi-Wan got a reaction. Only it wasn't one he was expecting. The professor smiled evilly, his decaying, yellow teeth showing themselves. The expression appeared frozen on his face. No matter how he tried, Obi-Wan couldn't figure out what the smile meant.

Obi-Wan felt frustration again. Lundi was like a blank wall. Though he was weaker than when Obi-Wan had first seen him ten years ago on Coruscant, his mind was a puzzle. Obi-Wan could not access his thoughts, even with the Force. How could he determine who was seeking the Holocron if the Quermian wouldn't cooperate?

"Norval was on Kodai with you," Obi-Wan said in a loud voice. The echo it made in the hold surprised both him and Lundi, who looked up. Obi-Wan suddenly thought he might have found a way through the professor's wall.

"As was Omal. You were all after the Holocron together."

Lundi leaned forward, as if about to speak. His face was pressed against the bars of his cage. But a moment later he sat back again, smiling smugly.

"You had the knowledge, but you needed these children to do your dirty work. To actually get it for you. You didn't think you could dive that deep alone . . ."

Obi-Wan desperately waited for Lundi to jump in, to begin talking, to object to what he was saying. But the professor seemed to know that was exactly what Obi-Wan wanted. He sat there like a stone, all of his long arms folded across his chest. His face was contorted into a defiant sneer.

Obi-Wan suddenly felt the urge to break through the cage's bars and rip the sneer right off Lundi's face. Even insane and locked in a cage, the Quermian had power. And at that moment, Obi-Wan hated that power with every fiber of his being.

"We need to know if the Holocron is still in the crater!" he shouted. "We need to get to it before —"

Obi-Wan stopped himself. In his anger, he'd almost blurted out dangerous information. Having been locked up for the last ten years,

Lundi wouldn't know that the Sith had actually returned. He wouldn't know that others in the galaxy possessed the knowledge he'd sought. . . .

Lundi's tiny head tilted to one side. "You are afraid, boy. But not of my students," he said, leaning forward again. "No . . . there's something more. Something much bigger, much more horrifying." He spoke slowly, as if he wanted to make sure Obi-Wan caught every word. "The Sith," he said, sitting back again. His eye widened and Obi-Wan could see his large, black pupil. "You are afraid of the Sith, of their return."

Lundi sat back and cackled loudly. "You should be," he said.

Obi-Wan gazed steadily at Lundi. He knew the professor wanted him to say something, to acknowledge his fear. He wouldn't give him that satisfaction.

The hold was completely silent for several long minutes as the two stared at each other. Finally, Lundi spoke.

"I can tell you where the Holocron is," he said, sounding remarkably lucid. "I can even tell you how to get it. The question is, what can you do for me in return?"

CHAPTER 18

Anakin circled the ship for the third time. He hadn't seen anything unusual and was beginning to think that the captain was just being paranoid. Given his personality, it certainly seemed possible. And, Anakin had to admit, hanging around with Dr. Lundi could be unsettling for anyone.

Satisfied that nothing was amiss, he headed into the vessel. Obi-Wan was on the bridge programming the Kodai coordinates into the navsystem.

"We're heading to Kodai immediately," he said. Anakin was relieved to be leaving the planet and moving ahead. His Master, too, seemed pleased.

"The professor finally confirmed that the Holocron is still in its undersea vault."

Anakin wrinkled his nose. "He could be lying," he pointed out.

Obi-Wan sighed. "I know," he admitted. "He might be trying to put us in danger. Or he could be toying with us. But it is the only information we have to go on, and my instinct is telling me that we should trust it. Besides, we only have the short time during the low tide to check."

Anakin nodded. He was feeling better about the hologram message now that they were about to leave the planet. Perhaps it was a good time to tell Obi-Wan about it.

"Master," he began. "I found some —"

"I'm telling you, somebody was out there," the pilot said, interrupting him. "Someone was messing with my ship."

Anakin rolled his eyes before turning to the captain. The guy was beginning to get on his nerves.

"I checked everything out," Anakin said reassuringly. "Everything looked just fine."

The captain looked doubtful but didn't reply as the ship took off. Soon they could only see the blackness of space through the cockpit viewscreen. The captain prepared for hyperspace.

Anakin suddenly felt tired and was grateful for a bit of downtime. The trip to Kodai would take more than a day, so he'd have a little while to rest and collect his thoughts.

Suddenly there was a loud explosion on the engine side, and the ship rocked hard to the left.

"I told you!" the captain screamed. "Some-one has sabotaged my ship. We have to land immediately!"

"We can't," Obi-Wan said rationally. "That is exactly what the saboteurs would want us to do."

The captain's eyes went wide. "But we can't fly like this," he said, his voice rising while smoke poured into the cockpit from the rear of the ship. "My controls are useless. We'll all die."

Anakin felt annoyance rise in him again. But this time it was mixed with a sense of guilt. Someone *had* obviously tampered with the ship, in spite of the fact that he initially didn't believe the captain's concerns.

"Nobody is going to die," Anakin said calmly. "Just show me where you keep your tools."

The captain pointed to a small cupboard right outside the cockpit. Anakin retrieved the kit and moved to the back of the ship, waving his hands to clear the smoke. The flames had been extin-guished by automatic fire controls and the dam-aged engine was accessible through a large hatch in a rear corridor. Though Anakin could fix it, it would not be easy while the ship was in motion.

Anakin opened the hatch and saw immedi-ately that the circuitry bay had been fused. That meant that several circuits needed to be replaced — and fast. The question was, which ones? Some were trivial, and others would repair the ship enough for it to fly to Kodai.

Anakin was not particularly familiar with the kind of ship they were on. He'd never flown one before, and certainly never repaired one. He'd have to follow his instincts.

Pulling out a light energy tool, he got to work on the circuitry wires. It was difficult to hold the tool steady, since the ship was banking in all directions. Working carefully, he reconnected the damaged wires one by one. Soon the ship stabilized, and the pilot once again had control.

Anakin repaired a few more wires and closed the hatch. On his way back to the cockpit he passed Lundi's cage.

"Nice work, young one," the professor said. "I could have used you on Kodai."

Anakin tried to ignore the comment as he replaced the tools in the cupboard. The Quermian was loony, and said crazy things all the time.

"Good job, Padawan," Obi-Wan said proudly as Anakin entered the cockpit.

"We can make it to Kodai now," the captain said. "Though it may take a bit longer than originally scheduled."

The relief in the cockpit was palpable. They were all safe — for the moment.

CHAPTER 19

Obi-Wan studied his Padawan as he put away the tool kit. He was relieved that he'd fixed the engine, of course. But as he watched his apprentice, Obi-Wan also experienced another feeling — worry.

When Obi-Wan had started this mission with Qui-Gon ten years earlier, he'd been troubled by the dark side. He'd felt frustrated, vulnerable, and afraid.

Anakin did not appear to be feeling any of these things. No, it was something else.

Obi-Wan saw the boy walk up to Lundi's cage and stare at the Quermian. He did not show any fear. Instead he seemed . . . fascinated.

His Padawan was extremely curious about Lundi and what had turned him into an insane criminal. In fact, he seemed drawn toward the power that had corrupted Lundi and Omal.

This curiosity worried Obi-Wan.

Of course Anakin had not seen the power of the dark side the way that Obi-Wan had. He had not witnessed his Master being cut down by a Sith Lord. He had not been nearly killed himself.

After such a close experience Obi-Wan was well aware of the threat the Sith posed if they regained all of their ancient power. And recapturing the knowledge contained in a Sith Holocron would be a large step in that direction. It could be devastating for the entire galaxy.

Obi-Wan shuddered at the thought before letting it fade to the back of his mind. He needed to sharpen his focus and bring his attention back to the moment, and his Padawan.

The boy needed guidance, Obi-Wan knew. A decade earlier, his own Master had skillfully led him in the right direction — away from anger and frustration. It had kept Obi-Wan firmly on the Jedi path. When Qui-Gon died, Obi-Wan had promised to give that guidance to Anakin.

Obi-Wan remembered Anakin's angry outburst at Lundi when they were first on the ship. Anger was dangerous. Perhaps he should be warning his apprentice about the dark side — that it was an easy path to power, but also to self-destruction.

The problem was, he did not know how to put the words together. He did not know exactly what to say. And whenever he offered Anakin this kind of guidance, the boy brushed it aside. It was almost as if Anakin thought that the things Obi-Wan was trying to warn him about did not apply to him.

With a sigh, Obi-Wan wished that Qui-Gon were still alive. He would know just what to say, what to do. He would be able to get through to Anakin.

"I think we're being followed," the pilot said after they came out of hyperspace, breaking into Obi-Wan's thoughts.

Obi-Wan rose and approached the controls. It was not unlikely, he realized. Whoever sabotaged the ship could easily be on their tail.

Obi-Wan carefully searched the ship's detection system. He found nothing.

Soon they landed safely on Kodai. After instructing the pilot not to leave the planet, Obi-Wan led Anakin downtown.

"We need to get to the water soon," Obi-Wan explained as they made their way up the main street. The tide was already going out, but they weren't going to wait for it to hit its lowest point. If they did, they might be too late; they had to beat Norval, or whoever was after the Holocron. This time they had to get there first.

Anakin looked around. "There's not much here, is there?" he asked.

"No," Obi-Wan replied. "There was a huge

tidal wave several hundred years ago, and many Kodaians were killed. Most of the survivors fled the planet. Those who remain await another giant wave, and in their minds, certain death."

Anakin grimaced. "That's pretty bad," he said.

Obi-Wan laughed. "I agree, Padawan." Then his expression grew serious. "I would not choose to live my life in such a way. But the Kodaians did not choose, either. It would be difficult to have a history of loss."

Anakin was thoughtful as they scoured the town. "You'd think there'd be diving shops everywhere," he finally said. "Practically the whole planet is sea."

"True. But the people are afraid of it," Obi-Wan reminded him.

"They seem afraid of us, too," Anakin said. "Whenever we pass someone, they move more quickly and look away."

"You are observant, Anakin," Obi-Wan said proudly. "Kodaians do not feel comfortable around strangers."

After checking the tide and finding it was not yet the right time to dive, the Jedi made their way back to the ship. Many Kodaians went out of their way to avoid them on the streets. Others stopped to stare at them. And a few shouted warnings about the deadly sea and its hidden evils.

"Master," Anakin suddenly said. His voice was quiet, almost hesitant. This was unusual for the boy. "I have something to tell you."

Obi-Wan stopped and turned toward his Padawan. "What is it?" he asked.

"I found a holoprojector when we were at Omal's apartment. It . . . it had a message on it, one of the messages Master Ki-Adi Mundi told us about."

Obi-Wan's eyes widened. "A message showing a Jedi being killed?" he asked.

Anakin nodded.

For a moment Obi-Wan did not know how to respond. This was important information — not something an apprentice should keep from his Master.

"Why didn't you tell me before?" he asked in a raised voice.

"I . . . I didn't think it was important," Anakin mumbled. "We already knew the messages existed, and you wanted to get back to the ship."

Obi-Wan stared at his Padawan. He never would have considered keeping this kind of information from Qui-Gon. As a Jedi team, it was essential that they share every piece of knowledge they gathered. They had to trust each other. Completely.

With a jolt, Obi-Wan realized that Anakin

might not totally trust him. Why else would he keep something like this from him?

As Obi-Wan stared down at his Padawan learner, an awful thought crept into his mind: He wasn't sure he completely trusted Anakin, either.

"You should have told me immediately," Obi-Wan said sternly. "Be sure that you do so next time."

Anakin looked down at his feet. "Yes, Master," he said.

Without another word, Obi-Wan turned away and continued down the street.

The Jedi were silent as they walked back to the ship. Inside, Dr. Lundi was asleep in his cage, his loud snores filling the hold. He woke abruptly when the Jedi entered.

"Can't a prisoner get some sleep around here?" he grumbled, wiping a line of drool off his chin with one hand and rubbing his eye with another.

"Not when he has agreed to provide important information," Obi-Wan replied flatly. "I need you to answer some questions about your last journey to the bottom of the Kodaian sea. It's time for you to tell us what you know."

The professor glared at Obi-Wan for several long seconds. It was true that he had agreed to answer questions in exchange for the chance to look upon the Holocron once more. "Go on," he finally said.

"Ten years ago you came to Kodai to go after the Holocron," Obi-Wan said. "And one of your star pupils came after you."

"Norval," Lundi said, nodding. "He *was* my star pupil. Had such a hunger for knowledge."

"Dark knowledge," Obi-Wan noted, looking pointedly at Dr. Lundi.

Lundi shrugged. "It is not my responsibility how the boy used what he learned. I was only the teacher. I simply passed the information along."

Lundi's casual response made Obi-Wan angry. He obviously took his powerful position as a teacher very lightly. Didn't he understand the effect he had on people? Didn't he know he was responsible for the destruction of at least one young life?

"But Norval was strong — stronger than even I knew," Lundi went on. "He got to the Holocron first. He brought it up still inside its vault. We fought over it, and it fell into the geyser crater."

Obi-Wan closed his eyes as disappointment surged inside him. Though he'd known that the Holocron could have fallen deeper into the pocketed seafloor, he'd hoped it wasn't true. It meant that the Holocron was *very* far down.

And located inside a gushing geyser that was incredibly treacherous, even at the lowest tide.

The Holocron could easily be so far down that no one would be able to retrieve it. But what if it wasn't?

Obi-Wan was not feeling confident about anything on this mission. Yet he had no choice but to move forward — before someone else did.

CHAPTER 20

Anakin squinted into the darkness as the loaded gravsled zoomed over the exposed sea-floor. The tide was already partially out, and soon they would be traveling over the water.

"That way," Obi-Wan said, pointing off to the left. They were the first words he'd spoken to him since their argument. Anakin felt badly about not telling his Master about the hologram message sooner, but wasn't sure why it was such a big deal. He did tell him, didn't he?

Anakin turned the vehicle. Beside him, Dr. Lundi was staring through the bars of his portable cage. His eyes were wide, and he couldn't sit still. He seemed like an excited child.

He can't wait to see the Holocron, Anakin thought. The ancient artifact had quite a reputation to live up to. As he increased the gravsled's speed, the young Jedi secretly hoped that it would.

The gravsled zoomed over the water, heading straight toward the crater. Anakin thought he saw something sticking up above the shallow sea. It looked like a diving platform.

"Just ahead," Obi-Wan said. Anakin could hear the disappointment in his Master's voice. He pulled the gravsled up beside a platform piled with equipment and cut the engine.

Obi-Wan stared down at the water suit and air tank. "Someone has already been here," he said. "I only hope they haven't found the Holocron."

Anakin scanned the surface of the sea. He could feel a powerful, dark energy surrounding them. But he wasn't sure if it was because the Holocron was still below, or because it had been there for years.

"The Holocron is gone," Lundi cackled. He waved his arms, smacking several against the top and sides of his travel cage. "He came back. Norval's got it."

Obi-Wan pulled on his breather and gestured for Anakin to do the same. In spite of Lundi's words, the Jedi couldn't leave this time until they were certain that the Holocron was not still under the sea. After checking to make sure that

Lundi's cage was anchored securely to the gravsled, they dove into the water.

Obi-Wan led the way down the side of the crater to the rocky shelf below. It was a long way down and Anakin felt a surge of excitement as they dropped lower and lower. *This* was a mission.

Once they were on the shelf, it was easy to locate the geyser — a huge mass of hot water gushed out of it every several minutes. That didn't leave them much time to investigate what was below.

Anakin dove down into the crater after his Master, kicking as hard as he could. There was nothing in front of him except the inky blackness of the deep sea. He could barely see his Master's legs moving back and forth just a few meters in front of his face. At last Obi-Wan lit a glow rod.

Down, down, down they swam. Anakin's ears popped several times from the pressure, and the water got warmer and warmer.

After what seemed like several minutes, Anakin caught a glimpse of a sinister red glow several meters in front of them, rising from the seafloor. His breath caught in his throat as he came to a halt. The water here seemed to pulsate with energy, and he had to concentrate to stay in one place. The same appeared to be true for his Master.

Obi-Wan gestured for Anakin to stay put and cautiously swam forward toward a glowing vault. Anakin saw his legs move back and forth, then stop. Obi-Wan thrust his glow rod into the tomblike box. It was empty. A second later Obi-Wan had turned around and was pointing up. He wanted Anakin to head back to the surface.

Anakin wondered how long they'd been down there. Five minutes? Six? There wasn't much time before the geyser would blow again.

Turning around as quickly as he could, he bolted for the surface. But swimming up was not easy. It almost felt as if something was holding him down, keeping him in the geyser. Kicking hard, he moved slowly upward.

Anakin's legs were aching when he felt a small gush of warm water rush past him. With a series of furious kicks, he surged ahead. He did not want to be anywhere nearby when the geyser erupted.

Finally the geyser walls disappeared and the Jedi were once again in open water. Sprinting forward, they moved away from the geyser mouth just as a giant burst of scalding water shot out.

The Jedi wasted no time getting back to the

gravsled. Now that they knew the Holocron was not there, they had to get back to civilization as soon as possible.

Anakin pulled off his breather and started the gravsled. They were practically moving when Obi-Wan climbed out of the water.

"It was gone," Lundi declared, looking at the Jedi's empty hands. "Clever. The boy is clever — more clever than I thought. I should have suspected. Yes, suspected. He almost had it the last time, he did. Until Omal got in his way. Lucky for me. Unlucky for him. Omal gave me a chance to attack — to get the Holocron for myself. But Norval was a formidable opponent. I have to hand it to him . . ."

Lundi's voice trailed off as he lost himself in the ten-year-old memory.

"Where would Norval take the Holocron?" Obi-Wan asked.

Professor Lundi crossed several arms across his chest. "A deal, a deal," he said defiantly. "We had our deal. I told you secrets for a chance to see the Holocron. But I didn't see it, did I? The game is up, up, up. And you lost. The boy has the Holocron. The boy. Ha!"

Anger swelled inside Anakin. He waited for his Master to do something, to shake some sense into the old loon. But Obi-Wan was silent as he stared glumly at the professor.

Wearing a sinister smirk, Lundi looked from Anakin to Obi-Wan. "Though I doubt the boy actually knows what to do with it," he added under his breath. "But at least he's not cowardly like you and the rest of your robed friends."

That's it. Anakin switched off the gravsled and lunged at the professor. He could smell the old Quermian's rancid breath as he leaned in close to his face.

"This isn't funny, wormhead," he said furiously. "Your boy may not know what to do with the Holocron, but the Sith will."

The smile disappeared from Professor Lundi's face as he stared back at Anakin. He dropped all of his gangly arms to his sides.

"I suspect you know your history, professor," Anakin shouted, forcing the Quermian's long neck farther and farther back. "And that you're well aware if the Sith gain power it's not just the Jedi who will die."

CHAPTER 21

Obi-Wan looked back and forth between Anakin and Dr. Lundi. He knew that Anakin's outburst was not appropriate. It was not the Jedi way, and Anakin seemed to let anger overtake him too easily. Obi-Wan could still see a flicker of fury in his eyes. As his Master, it was his duty to reprimand the boy for his behavior. To counsel him about the danger of negative emotions.

But the outburst seemed to have an effect on Lundi. For the first time since they'd left Coruscant, the professor appeared cowed. The young Jedi had actually managed to intimidate Professor Lundi. For this Obi-Wan was grateful.

Obi-Wan watched his Padawan return to the controls and start the gravsled engine.

He is so different from me, he thought. *Our relationship is so different from the one I shared with Qui-Gon.*

Of course with Anakin, Obi-Wan was no longer

the Padawan. He was the Master, and it was his job to lead, to teach. He often found himself wondering if he was ready for this awesome responsibility. It had all happened so fast — one day he was a Padawan learner himself, and the next he was Anakin's Master. He could not help but feel that it was really a role for Qui-Gon.

Like Qui-Gon, Anakin had a tendency to break the rules. He often chose to follow his instincts instead of the Jedi code. But his decisions, while sometimes rash, almost always got results. They almost always put the mission a step ahead, and often left Obi-Wan at odds.

This is not the time for a reprimand, Obi-Wan thought as they sped back toward shore. They had to get to the hangar before Norval rounded up transport and left the planet altogether.

Within a few minutes the gravsled was at the hangar. But their hired ship and its pilot were nowhere to be seen.

"He's fled," Obi-Wan said, grimly looking around the hangar.

"That coward," Anakin said with disgust. "I never should have fixed his ship. The next time I see him —"

"We don't have time to deal with that now," Obi-Wan interrupted. "Let's find out who has left the planet in the last few hours and see if we can track them."

After securing the still-silent Lundi's cage to a hangar wall, Obi-Wan and Anakin split up to search the hangar. Obi-Wan had seen Norval ten years earlier, and had described him to his Padawan. But aside from an average-sized young man with dark hair, they didn't have much to go on.

The hangar was not particularly busy, and none of the pilots Obi-Wan approached had seen Norval — or at least they said they hadn't seen him. If they said anything at all. Disappointed, Obi-Wan decided to check the hangar records.

Only one ship had left in the last few hours. It was headed toward the Ploo Sector. But no planet was specified.

"Did you find anything?" Anakin asked as he approached his Master. "Nobody would talk to me."

"Just this," Obi-Wan said, tossing Anakin the records. It seemed that the Holocron had eluded him a second time. Trying to find a mystery ship in a vast sector was a long shot, and it was all they had to go on.

"Why would he go to the Ploo Sector?" Anakin asked.

Several meters away, Lundi stuck his narrow head through the bars of his cage. "Norval was a good student. A great one. In fact the only thing that surpassed his desire for knowledge and power was his greed." Dr. Lundi stood up as straight as he could inside his cage. "I was offered vast riches by several anonymous parties to turn over the Sith Holocron should I ever capture it. One of the parties wanted to rendezvous beside my home planet of Ploo II."

The Jedi exchanged glances. Should they believe him? Lundi had several reasons to thwart their progress. He probably enjoyed the idea of Norval having the Holocron, of his using it for his own evil uses. He would take pride in that. Norval was, after all, Lundi's prize student.

But for the first time Obi-Wan felt he had some insight into Lundi's thoughts. It was as if a wall had been torn down, and Obi-Wan sensed that the professor was telling the truth. The Quermian wanted to go after the Holocron himself. He wanted a chance to see it again, to be close to its power.

"We need a ship to get us to Ploo II," Obi-Wan said. "Quickly."

CHAPTER 22

According to the flight records, the ship that left for the Ploo Sector was very large and not particularly fast. Anakin knew that if they were going to catch it, they'd need a fast vehicle with a powerful hyperdrive.

There was only one such ship in the hangar. The pilot looked at the Jedi warily as they approached.

"Ploo II?" he repeated with disdain. "No thanks. I just got here, and won't be doing anything but taking a nice long rest."

"I can pilot," Anakin said. "You can even stay here and rest. We'll bring the ship back when we're finished."

The pilot looked at Anakin as if he were crazy. Anakin couldn't blame him. If it were his ship, he wouldn't let some stranger take it off planet, either. Not even a Jedi.

But they needed the ship. Badly.

Obi-Wan waved his hand in front of the pilot's face. "You can trust us to borrow the ship," he said slowly.

"I guess I can trust you to borrow the ship," the pilot said.

"We will bring it back when we are finished," Obi-Wan added.

"Just bring it back when you are finished," the pilot echoed.

Anakin grinned. They weren't lightsabers, but Jedi mind tricks really came in handy sometimes.

"I'll get Lundi," Obi-Wan said.

Anakin nodded and boarded the ship. From the pilot's seat he plugged in the coordinates for Ploo II. Minutes later Obi-Wan and Lundi were on board, and the ship was heading into the atmosphere.

Anakin thought he might have a chance to talk to Obi-Wan on the way, but Obi-Wan silently left the cockpit shortly after they had taken off. Anakin guessed that he was still upset.

Trying not to think about it, Anakin studied the computer's programmed hyperdrive route. If there was a faster way to get there, he wanted to know about it. They had to catch the Holocron thief.

There appeared to be only one direct route,

and the computer had chosen it. Anakin engaged the hyperdrive, and the nearby stars streaked by in flashes of blinding light.

Once the ship was safely in hyperspace, Anakin could step away from the controls and relax a bit. Moving into the hold, he saw that the professor was sound asleep. He'd been sleeping a lot lately, and as Anakin studied him he appeared older and more frail. His body shuddered with every breath. It seemed as if his life forces were ebbing.

Asleep and helpless in his cage, the professor seemed more pitiful than threatening. Anakin almost felt sorry for him. But then, the Quermian had not made this mission an easy one. He had been difficult from the start, and the way he'd treated his Master had infuriated Anakin.

Now, under his direction, they were chasing a ship on its way to Ploo II. Was it the right planet, or were they simply on a fruitless chase? It would be so easy for Lundi to lead them astray. After being locked up by Jedi for ten years, it was entirely possible that he was out for revenge. Anakin couldn't really blame him for wanting to take his imprisonment out on someone.

Anakin watched Lundi sleep for a long time and tried to meditate. He was left with many questions about Dr. Lundi and the Holocron.

But he didn't think that the professor was lying to them about following Norval. Anakin sensed that they were closing in on something powerful and evil . . . and believed it to be the Holocron.

Anakin got to his feet and moved toward the pilot's seat. It was almost time to bring the ship out of hyperspace. Sitting down at the controls, he suddenly felt a ripple in the Force. He quickly brought the ship out of lightspeed. The familiar starriness of space came into view around him.

But that was not the only thing Anakin saw.

Obi-Wan was beside him in an instant. "I felt a wave in the Force," he said.

Anakin pointed to a sleek gray ship visible in the viewscreen.

"It just passed us," he said.

"Whose ship is it?" Anakin asked, wide-eyed.

Obi-Wan sighed. "I don't know," he confessed. "But I have a feeling we'd better get to Norval's ship before it does."

The large ship shuddered. Anakin had been pushing it hard since they'd sighted the sleek gray vessel, and wasn't sure how much longer it would hold up. The speed they were flying at was certainly faster than the craft was accustomed to. By the time they landed somewhere it would probably need repairs.

The mysterious gray ship was now in front of them and had slowed down.

Anakin's Master stood beside him with his eyes closed. "I feel something powerful, but it could be coming from that ship and not the Holocron. We've got to locate Norval quickly. I have a hunch that whoever is aboard that ship is after the Holocron too.

"I'll keep an eye out," Anakin assured his Master. "Why don't you prepare a shuttle. When I find his ship you can be ready to board immediately."

Obi-Wan nodded at Anakin gratefully. "Monitor all ship-to-ship communications and let me know if you sense anything unusual."

While Obi-Wan prepared a shuttle, Anakin carefully circled the gray ship in a wide arc.

Anakin was just coming around the gray ship when another, larger ship came into view in the space lane. Anakin felt instantly certain that it was Norval's. There was a strange flutter in his stomach, like nausea.

Anakin switched on his comlink. "I see another ship," he reported. "And I'm feeling kind of weird. I'll bet the Holocron is in there."

"Good. I'm closing the shuttle hatch now," Obi-Wan said. "Activate the shuttle bay doors immediately."

Anakin pressed a button on his control panel

and Obi-Wan's shuttle shot out of the ship. It looked tiny as it hurtled toward Norval's massive vessel. Anakin hoped it would land safely on Norval's ship without being detected by the mysterious gray craft.

As Anakin watched the shuttle approach Norval's ship, a voice spoke up behind him. Lundi.

"Too late, too late," he murmured.

Anakin turned around and saw that Lundi's eyes were closed. Was he asleep, or awake?

Too late for what? Anakin wondered.

He didn't have long to ponder. Just then a huge blast rocked the ship.

CHAPTER 23

From the small window in the tiny shuttle, Obi-Wan saw a red blast explode against Anakin's ship. The gray vessel had finally detected their ship and was clearly not pleased about its presence.

The sight of the red laser triggered something in Obi-Wan's memory, and a familiar feeling of helplessness washed over him. But there was no way he could get back to the ship fast enough to help his Padawan. And there was the Holocron. He had to go after it while he had the chance. He would not leave it behind again.

Obi-Wan quickly sent a mental message to his Padawan. *You can do it, Anakin,* he told him. *Just think carefully . . .*

Within minutes the shuttle locked into the docking bay on Norval's ship. After powering down the tiny craft, Obi-Wan quietly slipped out into the bigger ship.

As he moved down a glistening white corridor, the sound of more laser fire echoed in Obi-Wan's ears. Anakin's ship was getting pounded. Obi-Wan suddenly wished he and his Padawan had resolved their discussion on Kodai.

You can't do anything about that now, he told himself. He had to focus and think clearly if he was going to find the Holocron on this giant craft.

Obi-Wan hurried down several sterile corridors. As he reached the end of one he suddenly felt something evil washing over him. He knew exactly how his Padawan had felt a few minutes earlier. The Holocron *was* close.

Obi-Wan rounded a corner and spotted a large room at the end of the passageway. A humanoid figure stood with its back to the door, waiting. And there, on a transparisteel table, sat the glowing red Holocron.

Obi-Wan approached the room carefully. But before he was through the door the figure turned toward him.

"I have been waiting for you," Norval said.

Obi-Wan focused hard on the dark-haired man in front of him as queasiness threatened to overtake him. He sensed that, in fact, he *wasn't* the person Norval had been waiting for. He'd been expecting someone else — Lundi, perhaps. Or whoever was piloting the sleek gray ship.

"Powerful, isn't it?" Norval cackled. "The nauseous feeling takes some getting used to. When you are comfortable with the power, it disappears."

Obi-Wan dove for the Holocron, but Norval quickly stepped in front of it.

"This information would be wasted in the hands of the Jedi," he spat. "You have no idea what to do with power."

Obi-Wan could see that Norval was not going to give up without a fight. Reaching down to his utility belt, he unhooked and ignited his lightsaber.

I must end this quickly, Obi-Wan thought. He hoped the sight of his lightsaber would make Norval back down and hand over the Holocron. *I must get back to help Anakin before it is too late.*

But Norval did not back down. He simply reached for his belt and ignited a lightsaber of his own.

CHAPTER 24

Anakin unleashed another round of laser fire. He'd been circling the sleek gray ship, pummeling its hull. Every blast appeared to find its quick-moving target. But they didn't seem to have any effect.

I should have chosen a ship with decent fire-power as well as speed, Anakin thought grimly. *I should have known I'd need to be prepared for battle.*

Anakin had taken several hits without sustaining much damage. Only that first firing had created a problem, and losing the hyperdrive was minor compared to what could have been damaged.

Still, the ship could be hit again at any moment — and with dire results. He had to get out of there. But where could he go? The large gray craft clearly had a long firing range. It would take several minutes to get far enough away to be safe. . . .

Thinking fast, Anakin turned the ship around and headed straight for Norval's behemoth. If he could just keep the giant vessel between him and the mystery ship, he'd count on the gray ship not firing on him. The pilot wouldn't want to risk the Holocron — he hoped.

Anakin breathed a sigh of relief when he saw that the gray ship was not coming after him. But before he could inhale again it turned its fire on Norval's ship. Somehow, the pilot knew the Jedi were getting close.

Obi-Wan gaped at the lightsaber in Norval's hand for half a second. Such a weapon was extremely difficult to construct, and doing so took patience and skill. Attributes he wasn't at all convinced that Norval had.

Norval stepped forward, his blade raised. He was clearly pleased to see the look of surprise on Obi-Wan's face.

"You Jedi think you are the only ones who can wield lightsabers?" he laughed menacingly. "Dr. Lundi's lessons only took me so far. But the Quermian did help me gather the tools I needed. It's actually quite simple, once you have the knowledge — and the power . . ."

Obi-Wan was barely listening. He circled Norval, carefully studying the lightsaber. Its construction was crude, and he guessed that the crystals inside were weak and badly tuned. At least he hoped that was the case.

Norval brought the weapon high over his head, then thrust it back down. It missed Obi-Wan by several centimeters and crashed into the table where the Holocron rested. The glowing artifact tumbled to the floor. Both Obi-Wan and Norval watched the Holocron fall, but neither made a move for it.

His lightsaber might be crude, but it is still deadly, Obi-Wan noted. He knew from experience that a powerful weapon could be even *more* dangerous in the hands of an unskilled user. He would have to tread carefully.

Norval's eyes glinted. "Did the Jedi like my messages?" he asked, moving slowly forward. "I thought they were appropriate. Imagine being able to bring down the pathetic Jedi and get rich doing it!"

Norval slashed at the air, his fury building. It was clear to Obi-Wan that the young man was strong, but not very technically advanced with the lightsaber.

Obi-Wan sprang ahead, slashing with his own blue blade and pushing Norval backward. He had no desire to kill Norval — he simply wanted to disarm him and take the Holocron. This fight was wasting valuable time.

Obi-Wan closed in. But before he could knock Norval's lightsaber out of his hands, another explosion caused the ship to bank sharply. Obi-

Wan fell backward, losing his grip on his lightsaber and hitting his head hard on the floor.

It was some seconds before his vision cleared. When it did, Norval was standing over him. Obi-Wan could feel the heat from the glowing lightsaber blade, which was trained on his throat.

"You didn't think I could actually get the Holocron, did you?" he gloated. "Nobody did. If only Omal hadn't interfered the first time, I would be even stronger now — and you and Dr. Lundi would be long dead."

Obi-Wan pretended to listen as Norval ranted. The longer he talked, the more time he'd have to formulate some sort of plan. Once Norval decided to strike, Obi-Wan would be out of time — perhaps permanently.

Out of the corner of his eye Obi-Wan saw his lightsaber rolling away from him. Beyond it was the glowing Holocron, still on the floor.

Norval raised his saber. But just as he began to bring it back down another blast pelted the ship. It took Norval a moment to steady himself.

That moment was all Obi-Wan needed. Reaching out with both hands, he used the Force to bring his lightsaber and the Holocron to him. He caught one in each hand as he leapt to his feet. Then, reigniting his lightsaber, he gracefully knocked Norval's weapon out of his hand and across the room. The crude handle shattered, and the interior crystals spilled across the floor.

Stunned, Norval climbed to his feet. "Your young Padawan would have made a wonderful Sith," he growled, his face contorting into an expression of rage. "Too bad he and that ship he's on are about to be destroyed by some friends of mine." He grinned. "They'll stop firing on me once they know you've been taken care of."

Obi-Wan wondered for a split second how Norval knew about Anakin. He supposed the evil young man made many things his business. But before he could consider the thought further, Norval lunged for the ship's communicator. "The Jedi has the Holocron!" he shouted. "You've got to get me out of here."

Obi-Wan turned and ran out of the room while Norval begged for help. The Jedi Master would not strike down an unarmed being. He would not leave his Padawan to face the mystery ship alone. And he would not be leaving without the Holocron this time.

CHAPTER 26

All around him, doors began to slide closed. Obi-Wan hit the ground running. Squeezing sideways, he was just able to make it through the door he'd entered earlier and into the corridor. The last thing he saw was Norval laughing at him, a sneer twisting the lower half of his face.

"You have no idea what you are up against," he shouted.

Obi-Wan raced back down the white corridors to the shuttle. The glowing Holocron cast an eerie red glow on the walls. Obi-Wan ignored the queasiness in his gut and the weakness in his legs. He had to get to Anakin.

Within minutes Obi-Wan was hurtling out of the shuttle bay in the tiny vessel. Pressing his face to the transparisteel, he scanned the space for a sign of Anakin's ship. He didn't see one. Nor did he see the gray vessel. The earlier laser fire had stopped completely.

Obi-Wan sat back, discouraged. He was quite sure he'd know if his Padawan had been killed — he would have felt it. But where was he?

Obi-Wan programmed the shuttle to travel close to Norval's ship. He needed cover for as long as possible.

The shuttle glided through space, around to the other side of Norval's ship. Still Obi-Wan saw nothing. He was just about to give up and launch himself away when he spotted the small borrowed craft sneakily hiding right next to Norval's vessel. Obi-Wan was relieved. The boy was smart.

As soon as the shuttle had docked on the borrowed ship, Obi-Wan opened the door and hurried to the cargo bays. He had to secure the Holocron before he did anything else. He wanted someplace safe, and as far away from Lundi as possible.

Obi-Wan carefully placed the artifact in an onboard vault, and was immediately relieved to have it out of his hands. But he knew he wouldn't be completely comfortable until it was safely locked away in the Jedi archives on Coruscant . . . and perhaps not even then.

Obi-Wan rushed onto the bridge, eager to see his Padawan. But what he saw from the doorway was so surprising it stopped him in his tracks.

The professor's cage was empty and its door hung open. Anakin sat on the floor. He was cradling Lundi in his lap.

"I understand now," Lundi said in a hoarse whisper. "Some things are better left at the bottom of the sea."

Lundi gasped for air, and Obi-Wan suddenly realized that the Quermian was dying. He stepped forward and looked briefly into his eye. He finally saw what he'd always hoped he'd see — remorse and fear.

"I just . . . just hope it's not too late," Lundi finished. His fragile body shuddered and went limp, and Anakin laid him gently on the floor. Dr. Murk Lundi was dead.

Several emotions clashed inside Obi-Wan. Confusion, frustration, relief . . .

Anakin turned to face him. "I knew he was going to die," he explained. "And I didn't think he should end his life in a cage. So I let him out. I thought it was the right thing to do." His face was full of worry, and Obi-Wan realized that he had probably upset the boy with his outburst on Kodai.

"It is all right, Padawan," Obi-Wan said, placing a hand on Anakin's shoulder. He had much to learn as a Jedi Master, he realized. And it had taken him and Qui-Gon years of working together to develop their strong ties of trust.

Those ties would develop for him and Anakin as well, in time. As for Lundi, it didn't matter now. The Quermian and his evil were gone.

Obi-Wan saw relief wash over Anakin's young face. "I'm sorry about the hologram message," he said. "I didn't mean to keep it from you, I just —"

Obi-Wan nodded. "I know," he said. "I should not have reacted so strongly. Next time we will both do better."

"I hope there —" Anakin was suddenly interrupted by a flash of blinding light, followed by an earsplitting roar. The ship hurtled backward as debris pummeled the exterior.

"Cut the power," Obi-Wan barked.

Anakin raced to the controls and flipped the master switch. A second later they were enveloped in darkness. If they were lucky they would hurtle away with the flaming wreckage unnoticed by the mysterious gray ship —

Obi-Wan held his breath. He reached out to the Force and felt immediately that Norval was dead. The poor clever student was wrong. Whoever was aboard the gray ship was not his friend. The blast had been intended for the Jedi, and whoever had caused the fiery explosion had been willing to kill an ally to keep the Sith Holocron out of Jedi hands.

CHAPTER 27

The ship docked in the Coruscant hangar and Anakin and Obi-Wan disembarked. They'd drifted for hours while they patched the hyperdrive back together. Even with Anakin's skills as a mechanic they'd only just managed to limp the craft home. Now, there was much to do.

"I will see about getting the ship back to Kodai," Anakin offered.

Obi-Wan nodded. He had removed the Holocron from the cargo bay and was eager to get it to its permanent home in the archives. He'd learned to ignore the nausea, but would never be comfortable around this kind of dark power.

"Come to the Council Chambers when you are finished," Obi-Wan said. "I am sure the Council will want to hear from us as soon as possible."

Anakin nodded. "And Lundi?" he asked.

"I will have his body removed from the ship and brought into the Temple. The Council will decide what to do with him."

Obi-Wan watched Anakin cross the hangar, then hurried to the Jedi Temple. Jocasta Nu was waiting for him, the safe for the Holocron already open. They placed the artifact inside, then sealed the door and lowered it into the archive vault.

When the Holocron was out of view, Obi-Wan sighed in relief. He hoped he would never have to see or touch that evil object again.

By the time Obi-Wan arrived outside the Council Chambers door, Anakin was waiting for him. The boy smiled broadly as the Chambers door slid open.

"Congratulations," Depa Billaba said as they stepped inside. "A job well done."

"Indeed," agreed Saesee Tiin.

Anakin's eyes were lit with excitement. "It was a great mission," he said. "The most exciting one yet."

Obi-Wan noticed that Yoda's eyes registered concern as they rested on the boy. But the other Council members seemed only pleased and relieved to have the Sith Holocron safe in the Temple archives.

"Make a mission great, excitement does not,"

Yoda said gravely. The wise Master looked over at Obi-Wan, and Obi-Wan felt a twinge of guilt. Did Yoda think he was failing as Anakin's Master? Was he concerned that he was not capable of leading the boy?

These were his own fears, of course. Qui-Gon had been such a wonderful teacher. He was brave, strong, and wise. A gifted leader.

Would Qui-Gon think I am failing Anakin? That the boy needs an older and wiser Master?

Qui-Gon had been dead for almost four years, yet Obi-Wan suddenly felt his Master's presence. He was grateful for that, and took comfort in it. But sometimes he felt the loss so strongly that his chest ached.

"We will see that the remains of Professor Lundi are properly attended to," Mace Windu said.

The mention of Lundi's name brought Obi-Wan back to the moment.

"Well done, Jedi," Ki-Adi Mundi said, smiling. "You may go." The other Masters were nodding in agreement.

As Obi-Wan followed his Padawan out of the chambers, several images flashed in his mind: Dr. Lundi's mad, contorted face; the crude drawing of the Sith Holocron; the strange gray ship and its mysterious passengers; the Holocron itself; and, for a brief moment, the anger he'd seen in Anakin's eyes. These were just a handful of many signs he had seen on this mission. Signs of things that would not easily be laid to rest. . . .

Visit www.scholastic.com/starwars

and discover

The Early Adventures of
Obi-Wan Kenobi and Qui-Gon Jinn

STAR WARS

JEDI APPRENTICE

☐ BDN 0-590-51922-0	#1: The Rising Force	$4.99 US
☐ BDN 0-590-51925-5	#2: The Dark Rival	$4.99 US
☐ BDN 0-590-51933-6	#3: The Hidden Past	$4.99 US
☐ BDN 0-590-51934-4	#4: The Mark of the Crown	$4.99 US
☐ BDN 0-590-51956-5	#5: The Defenders of the Dead	$4.99 US
☐ BDN 0-590-51969-7	#6: The Uncertain Path	$4.99 US
☐ BDN 0-590-51970-0	#7: The Captive Temple	$4.99 US
☐ BDN 0-590-52079-2	#8: The Day of Reckoning	$4.99 US
☐ BDN 0-590-52080-6	#9: The Fight for Truth	$4.99 US
☐ BDN 0-590-52084-9	#10: The Shattered Peace	$4.99 US
☐ BDN 0-439-13930-9	#11: The Deadly Hunter	$4.99 US
☐ BDN 0-439-13931-7	#12: The Evil Experiment	$4.99 US
☐ BDN 0-439-13932-5	#13: The Dangerous Rescue	$4.99 US
☐ BDN 0-439-13933-3	#14: The Ties That Bind	$4.99 US
☐ BDN 0-439-13934-1	#15: The Death of Hope	$4.99 US
☐ BDN 0-439-13935-X	#16: The Call to Vengeance	$4.99 US
☐ BDN 0-439-13936-8	#17: The Only Witness	$4.99 US
☐ BDN 0-439-13937-6	#18: The Threat Within	$4.99 US

Also available:
☐ BDN 0-439-13938-4	Special Edition #1: Deceptions	$4.99 US

Scholastic Inc., P.O. Box 7502, Jefferson City, MO 65102

Please send me the books I have checked above. I am enclosing $_____ (please add $2.00 to cover shipping and handling). Send check or money order—no cash or C.O.D.s please.

Name_____ Birthdate_____

Address_____

City_____ State/Zip_____

Please allow four to six weeks for delivery. Offer good in U.S.A. only. Sorry, mail orders are not available to residents of Canada. Prices subject to change.

SWA202

© 2001 Lucasfilm Ltd. & TM. All rights reserved. Used under authorization.